Wishing & Hoping

"Well, I'd better get a move on. Here's your note-book," Jake said, handing it to Nancy. "See you later."

" 'Bye," Nancy said, and gave him the full treatment with her cool blue eyes.

Well, you kept it professional, Collins, but that woman sure does something to you, Jake thought to himself as he hurried out of Nancy's suite and down the stairs.

Once outside, Jake took in a deep lungful of the cool night air. He couldn't wait until the following evening. He imagined sitting next to Nancy in the darkened theater at the opening of *Grease!* and then afterward at the party, holding her close in his arms as they danced.

In his mind, they were the only two at the party.

NANCY DREW ON CAMPUS™

#1 New Lives, New Loves
#2 On Her Own
#3 Don't Look Back
#4 Tell Me the Truth
#5 Secret Rules
#6 It's Your Move

Available from ARCHWAY Paperbacks

For orders other than by individual consumers, Archway Books grants a discount on the purchase of **10 or more** copies of single titles for special markets or premium use. For further details, please write to the Vice-President of Special Markets, Pocket Books, 1230 Avenue of the Americas, New York, NY 10020.

For information on how individual consumers can place orders, please write to Mail Order Department, Paramount Publishing, 200 Old Tappan Road, Old Tappan, NJ 07675.

Nancy Drew
on campus™ #6

It's Your Move

Carolyn Keene

AN ARCHWAY PAPERBACK
Published by POCKET BOOKS
New York London Toronto Sydney Tokyo Singapore

The sale of this book without its cover is unauthorized. If you purchased
this book without a cover, you should be aware that it was reported to
the publisher as "unsold and destroyed." Neither the author nor the publisher has received payment for the sale of this "stripped book."

This book is a work of fiction. Names, characters, places and inci-
dents are products of the author's imagination or are used ficti-
tiously. Any resemblance to actual events or locales or persons,
living or dead, is entirely coincidental.

AN ARCHWAY PAPERBACK *Original*

An Archway Paperback published by
POCKET BOOKS, a division of Simon & Schuster Inc.
1230 Avenue of the Americas, New York, NY 10020

Copyright © 1996 by Simon & Schuster Inc.
Produced by Mega-Books, Inc.

All rights reserved, including the right to reproduce
this book or portions thereof in any form whatsoever.
For information address Pocket Books, 1230 Avenue
of the Americas, New York, NY 10020

ISBN: 0-671-52748-7

First Archway Paperback printing February 1996

10 9 8 7 6 5 4 3 2 1

NANCY DREW, AN ARCHWAY PAPERBACK and colophon
are registered trademarks of Simon & Schuster Inc.

NANCY DREW ON CAMPUS is a trademark of
Simon & Schuster Inc.

Cover photos by Pat Hill Studio

Printed in the U.S.A.

IL 8+

CHAPTER 1

"Watch it, babe!"

Nancy Drew jumped sideways as two beefy delivery men pushed past her, carrying 1950s-style chrome soda-fountain stools up the stairs to the porch of the Kappa sorority house.

What is all this? Nancy wondered. Another one of Kappa's pledge pranks? It looks like they're opening a restaurant.

"Coming through!" called one of the men. "Someone open the door!"

Nancy's close friend Bess Marvin threw open the door.

"Oh, wow! They look even better than when I saw them at the rental place." Bess motioned to the delivery men. "This way. Bring them into the back," she said excitedly, her blue eyes sparkling.

From the porch Nancy waved, catching Bess's attention. "Hi, Nan," Bess said distractedly, then turned to watch the progress of the stool delivery. "No, not back there. *That* way," she called, pointing to the dining room.

Nancy laughed as she ducked inside the Kappa house after the men. She was immediately flattened against the wall as several of Bess's sorority sisters raced through the hall with boxes loaded with straws and napkins.

"It's a danger zone around here," Nancy said.

"Don't mind them. C'mon, follow that chrome," Bess said, leading Nancy toward the dining room.

"Soda fountain stools?" Nancy asked, shaking her head. "I know Kappas really go all out for their parties, but decorations from a restaurant supply store? Pretty crazy!"

"Crazy is exactly what we're going for: 1950s crazy. We're doing a theme here for the opening night party tomorrow night," Bess said.

"Of course! *Grease!* is set in the 1950s," Nancy replied, smacking her forehead.

Bess grinned and pushed up the sleeves of her Wilder University sweatshirt. Then she consulted the clipboard she was carrying. "The stools are going to be seating for the party," she told Nancy. "They're cool, huh?"

Nancy nodded. "They're exactly right."

Kappa sorority was hosting the opening night party of Wilder University's Drama Department production of the musical *Grease!* Since Kappa was the house most noted for its involvement in the arts, it was the natural choice to put on the event.

Bess walked over to a counter that had been decorated to look like one in a 1950s soda fountain. "Set them down here," she said to the delivery men, indicating the area in front of the soda fountain.

Nancy examined the shiny metal napkin dispensers and old-fashioned condiment racks set on the counter.

"Everything looks great, doesn't it?" Bess asked. She plunked herself down on a seat and swiveled around.

Nancy smiled at her friend's enthusiasm and took a seat on another stool by the soda dispenser. She scanned the old-fashioned posters of cheeseburgers and malteds and thought how much this all reminded her of some of the old hangouts where she and Bess sometimes went in their hometown of River Heights.

"I just stopped by to say hi, but it looks like you guys could use some help," Nancy said.

Bess nodded as the men brought in another set of stools. "After we get these seats arranged, I could use some help with hanging old records from the ceiling. I don't have much time before rehearsal."

Moments later she and Nancy were sitting on the floor of the Kappa living room, combing through boxes of old records. Nancy dusted them off and handed them to Bess, who threaded fishing line through them. Around the room, several Kappa women were chatting and securing hooks into the ceiling.

"Boy, did you see those Sigma guys earlier today?" asked one girl with short dark hair.

"That's Devon." Bess laughed. In a louder voice she said, "Biggest flirt in our pledge class." The woman turned and gave Bess a mock scowl.

"That honor didn't go to you?" Nancy teased her friend.

Bess grinned. "Surprise, huh?" She tied an elaborate knot in the fishing line. "Okay, after we're finished putting string on these records, we'll hang them from the hooks in the ceiling."

Nancy glanced around. "I can't get over how you've transformed this whole place. I like the pennants you've hung everywhere, too," she said. "Talk about atmosphere. You've completely outdone yourselves."

"I hope so," another pledge said. "We don't need the upper-class sisters giving us a hard time."

Nancy turned to Bess. "Oh, come on. Would they really do that? You've all worked so hard."

"You'd be surprised," Bess murmured.

Just then a couple of upper-class sisters strode in casually, but Nancy could tell they were inspecting everything.

"We're going to hold the skit up there on that platform," Bess said, lowering her voice and jerking her chin toward the front of the room by the bay window.

"Skit?" Nancy looked puzzled.

Bess nodded. "Every year, the pledges have to perform a skit during a Kappa party."

One of the upperclasswomen looked over at Bess. "So what's the skit about, Bess?" she cajoled. "You can tell us."

"Not a chance," Bess replied, and whispered to Nancy, "Just my luck. This year they picked the opening night party to make us perform the skit. Here I am with a part in *Grease!* and I have to perform in a goofy pledge skit during my own opening night party." Bess sighed.

Nancy laughed. "I can't wait," she said. "I bet the skit will be the highlight of the party."

"Well, I *hope* it'll be good," Bess replied. "Come on, Nancy, I think they're ready for us to string these babies up."

Soon Nancy and Bess were perched on ladders, hanging records. As she worked, Nancy allowed her mind to wander to the next night's event, when she'd be back here with Jake Collins. Nancy shivered with anticipation.

Although she'd had lots of dates before, not to mention a longtime boyfriend, somehow Jake was different. He was a very cute junior who worked with her on the *Wilder Times,* the campus newspaper. This wasn't major romance material or anything yet. After her recent breakup with longtime boyfriend, Ned Nickerson, and a rocky romance with a guy named Peter Goodwin that never really got going, Nancy knew better than to jump feet first into another relationship. Still, she couldn't help noticing the way her stomach got fluttery whenever she thought of Jake. She closed her eyes and pictured herself dancing with him, her cheek resting lightly on his shoulder. . . .

"I can tell you've got Jake on the brain," Bess said.

"Oh, you think so?" Nancy replied, wondering if she really were that transparent.

"Yeah, I do," Bess said. "I've known you practically all my life, and I think I can tell when you've got a guy on your mind. It's this look you get."

"Hmmm," Nancy said.

Suddenly she saw that Bess had stopped stringing and let a record drop to the floor. "Oh, no," she said, glancing at her watch. "I'm late for rehearsal!"

"And I forgot I've got to meet George at the Student Union," Nancy added, carefully descending her ladder while holding the remaining records. "We've got some important shopping to do."

Bess was already off her ladder. "Say hi to my dear old cousin," she said. "And tell her I'll see her tomorrow night."

Nancy and Bess bolted from the Kappa house into the late afternoon sunshine, each headed in a different direction.

*　　*　　*

George Fayne pushed back her short, dark hair and gracefully slid her athletic body into a deep sofa in the Student Union. She glanced at her sports watch and saw that she was five minutes late. Frowning, she looked around the busy room and hoped Nancy hadn't come and gone already. There was a decidedly relaxed atmosphere this afternoon. Students were clustered together at low tables, some studying or chatting, others listening to headphones. George smiled as she saw her roommate, Pam Miller, and one of Nancy's suitemates, Eileen O'Connor, sitting and talking with several other students. George got up and took long strides over to their seating area.

"Hey," she greeted her friends. "How goes the battle?"

Pam looked up and smiled broadly at George. She whispered, "Back from your training run?" She turned to Eileen. "George is running in the Ten-K in a few weeks."

"Cool," Eileen said softly. She tilted her head to look up at George, her hair sweeping across her slightly freckled face. "Whew! I admire you. A Ten-K can be pretty grueling."

George grinned ruefully and rubbed her shin. "It's all for a good cause, so I'd better get in shape in a hurry. Since I've come to Wilder, I've pumped more than a few brain cells, but I've been neglecting my running legs in a big way." Once again she glanced around the Student Union. "Hey, you haven't seen Nancy anywhere,

7

have you? I'm supposed to meet her, but I was kind of late."

Eileen shook her head. "No, and we've been here for about an hour."

George noticed that a couple of students were frowning at her. What was their problem? And why was everyone whispering? "What's going on here?" she asked quizzically.

"We're part of the Intro to Political Theory class, and we're having an informal discussion," Pam whispered. She jerked her thumb in the direction of a good-looking woman wearing a long, dark skirt and a vest over a sweater. "Melina Stavros, the professor I was telling you about."

Intrigued, George watched the popular professor. She noticed Melina's dark good looks and assured demeanor as she masterfully commanded the area and drew out the students gathered around her, listening and commenting. When she spoke, Melina's husky voice reverberated with power. At once she was cajoling, demanding, and encouraging. Melina looks like a politician, George thought. The discussion soon moved on to the topic of the pros and cons of sororities and fraternities.

"I still think Alpha should have their charter revoked," declared one guy, who was sitting on the arm of Melina's chair. "They misused their power; therefore it should be stripped."

George wasn't surprised that the topic of Alpha Delta's hazing incident was still a hot topic around Wilder. A pledge named Tim Downing had suffered serious hypothermia during what was supposed to be a harmless pledge prank, and he was still recovering from the ordeal. George had leaned forward to hear what the other students thought when she saw Nancy making her way through the maze of students congregating in the Union.

She got up and pulled herself away from the discussion reluctantly, waving goodbye to her friends.

"Sorry, I've got to run," she whispered to Eileen. "Big shopping assignment in Weston. Nancy needs something to wow Jake Collins."

With that, George turned toward Nancy. She winced as she put weight on her left foot, and made a mental note to check her running shoes. Maybe while she was in Weston with Nancy, she'd check out the FleetFoot shoe store.

"Sorry I'm late," Nancy said breathlessly. "I was at the Kappa house helping Bess and forgot the time."

"No problem," George said. "I got to watch Pam's famous poli sci professor, Melina Stavros, in action. I usually don't get too involved in politics, but I have to admit, the discussion was pretty interesting with Melina leading it."

"Yes, I sat in on one of her classes once, since I'd heard so much about her," Nancy said. "She's got that great-sounding voice. I wish I had a deeper voice; it's powerful, and sexy." Nancy tugged George's sleeve. "Come on," she said, "let's go before all the stores are closed."

George had a feeling that at this moment Nancy didn't care one bit about Melina Stavros and her Intro to Political Theory class.

Eileen watched as Nancy and George disappeared through the Student Union doors and realized with a pang that although she was enjoying the spirited discussion going on around her, she'd much rather be heading off to the little university town of Weston with Nancy and George for a shopping trip. More than that, she wished she were going to the opening night of the play with some new guy she was crazy about. She'd been at college for several weeks and still hadn't had a university guy so much as look her way.

Eileen focused her thoughts back on the discussion about sororities and fraternities.

"It's unbelievable that something so elitist as the Greek system can still exist in the nineties," said a male student sitting near Melina.

"They're not all that elitist," Eileen retorted, wanting to defend the sorority house she was pledging. "I mean, anyone can rush, and if you play by the rules, you'll get picked by one house or another." She paused, aware of the looks she was getting. "Okay, so maybe it's not the house you'd choose, but no one ever said life was fair."

The male student snorted and sneered contemptuously at Eileen. "So then, you're saying, the frat system has cornered the market on unfairness," he said coolly.

"Don't forget the sororities," chimed in a woman sitting next to him. "I mean, I decided I might like to rush a sorority, but I was told no way—I'd missed the deadline; rush week had already started. Yet, a while later, along comes Casey Fontaine, Miss TV Star. Now, when Tall, Redheaded, and Gorgeous decides to rush a sorority, no one reminds *her* of any deadlines. I guess when a sorority decides it wants a celebrity, the rules aren't important."

Melina nodded. "Prestige has been the lifeblood of the Greek system. Do you think sororities feel justified in breaking rules to gain prestige? Maybe a celebrity feels she is above the rules and can muscle her way in wherever she wants?"

Eileen bristled. She wanted to jump up and let her classmates know that Casey hadn't been the one to approach the Kappa house. She hadn't "muscled" her way in. Still, Eileen knew that when it came right down to it, it really wasn't fair to people who had missed the deadline. She opened her mouth to speak but shut it again quickly. She could see how others might feel sororities and fraternities weren't exactly equitable.

Eileen sighed. She wished they weren't discussing this subject. She watched as two students nearby stole a quick kiss. Her attention wandered from the subject at hand as she started noticing how closely one or two of the guys sat next to a couple of girls. Practically everyone was paired off these days. Nancy off shopping for a dress to wow Jake. Her own roommate, Reva Ross, with her computer partner, Andy Rodriguez. Another suitemate, Ginny Yuen, and her boyfriend, Ray Johansson. The two-by-two list went on and on. Except for her. Eileen O'Connor had no one. It was depressing.

Suddenly Eileen had no taste for fraternities and sororities and the shifting balances of power. The only thing on her mind was shifting her boy-friendless state! Darting a sneaky glance into a compact mirror she had in her backpack, she frowned at her reflection. Boring brown hair. Freckle overload. Major blah. True, she wasn't unattractive, but she wished she had the startling good looks of someone like Casey Fontaine, which grabbed everyone's attention instantly.

Maybe, she reflected while the discussion grew in volume around her, she needed to participate more to be noticed. No, she decided. She *had* made a huge effort to become involved in university life. After all, she was here, wasn't she, participating in Melina's hot political debates outside of the lecture hall? And she was on the crew team and pledging Kappa, one of the most popular sororities on campus. It drew attention, even if it did draw fire in discussions like this.

"Is this seat taken?" whispered a deep male voice next to her.

Eileen was pulled from her thoughts as she gazed into the green eyes of a guy she'd noticed in her political theory lecture hall. He shot her a friendly grin as he plunked down on the armrest next to her. Eileen's shoulder burned as his jeans brushed against her.

"Paul Cody," Melina said by way of introducing the newcomer to the rest of the group. "Glad you could join us. We're discussing the mindset behind discrimination. Any insights on the subject?"

"Well, luckily for me, you're not discriminating against people who show up late for discussions," Paul said easily. The group laughed, and someone else jumped in with a comment.

Eileen felt him stare deeply into her eyes for a few seconds before he added quietly, "And you're not going to deny that I have equal rights to this chair even though you happened to get here first."

"N-No," Eileen said, feeling electric shivers go through her at his searing gaze. Hmm, she thought, feeling a renewed interest in the discussion. Paul may not know it yet, but he just might be the guy to help me end my single status here at Wilder!

"We're done," called Chris Vogel, the production assistant for *Grease!* "Chorus, stick around for a moment, we have to go over a couple of steps. The rest of you are dismissed."

Bess shivered as she stepped into the wings. Dress rehearsal had gone so well. She knew she should be wary—it was a well-known theater superstition that if a dress rehearsal went well, opening night was doomed. But Bess didn't have time for silly superstitions. Dress rehearsal had gone fabulously, and she had no doubt that they were in for an incredible opening night.

"Hey, Brian," she called to the good-looking, golden-haired young man who was in the chorus with her. "Way to go! That was some dancing."

Brian Daglian grinned uncertainly, revealing a row of straight white teeth. "Thanks," he said. "I was pretty nervous. I thought I was going to be sick and forget my two big lines, and it's only the dress rehearsal."

"So what? They say Sir Laurence Olivier was so nervous before his entrances that he threw up backstage," Bess said lightly, wanting to bolster Brian.

"I've got a long way to go before I can be spoken of in the same sentence as Olivier," Brian said. "But thanks."

He already looks like a movie star, Bess thought in a flash as Brian turned to talk with a couple of cast members. Bess took in his broad, leather-jacketed back. It was something about the way he moved. Brian had what their director called "presence." Although tonight Bess had to admit Brian *had* been a little off. Preperformance jitters, she decided. He'd be okay once the curtain went up the next day.

Impulsively, Bess hugged herself. *Grease!* was going to be a production Wilder students would remember for a long time, and she was thrilled to be part of it. All around her, the happy voices of her fellow actors flowed. Bess noticed that Casey Fontaine had joined Brian by the dressing room and was goofing around with him and some of the other cast members. Brian was doing a couple of the choreographed moves he would be performing.

"Hey, sorry, man," Bess heard Brian say a split second after his hand accidentally hit the shoulder of Erik Grenquist, a thin freshman who was carrying a stack of props.

Erik jerked his head up and shot Brian a venomous look that made Bess draw back in surprise. "Watch yourself," he snarled.

Brian started to grin, then stopped as he caught the glint in Erik's eye. "I said I was sorry," he said.

"Edgy," Bess heard Casey say.

"Jeez, everyone's nervous," Bess mumbled, and started to feel butterflies in her stomach. All of a sudden the good feelings from the dress rehearsal started to evaporate. What if the superstition was right and opening night was a flop?

"Now you're the one looking nervous," Brian said, coming over to her.

Bess laughed weakly. "Guess I am. I don't think I'll be able to sleep a wink tonight."

Just then Chris called the chorus members back to the stage.

Brian pushed back a lock of greased hair and took Bess's hand. "Tell you what. After we're done with this dance rehearsal, meet me by the stage door, and I'll give you a sci-fi video I borrowed from a friend. It's a total snore. You'll sleep like a baby, I guarantee it."

"I'll try anything," Bess said, nodding. "Even bad sci-fi."

"All right, Nancy," Kara Verbeck, Nancy's roommate, called out that evening. "Come on out. We're all waiting."

"Hold on a minute, I'm coming," Nancy said, emerging from her room and stepping into the lounge of Suite 301, where most of her suitemates were waiting eagerly. She was wearing a soft blue dress with a handkerchief hem and a low neckline.

"Wow," Kara gasped. "That's perfect! Wherever did you find that great shade of blue? Jake is going to die when he sees you!"

"That's gorgeous!" Liz Bader exclaimed. "I like the way it drapes."

Nancy grinned broadly and twirled around. "Thanks. The problem is, I can't figure out which shoes to wear with it."

"Shoes aren't your problem," Stephanie Keats

announced coolly, and Nancy braced herself for one of the cutting comments that the sophisticated-looking brunette was famous for delivering. But to Nancy's surprise, Stephanie only said, "What you need is a necklace or something to set it off."

"I've got just the thing!" Reva Ross said. The dark-skinned beauty jumped up from her chair and disappeared, reentering a minute later carrying a thin black cord with a small silver charm hanging from it.

"You can wear this tomorrow night if you want," she said, handing it to Nancy.

Nancy took the lovely necklace in her hand and squeezed Reva's shoulder. "Thanks. It's beautiful."

"You still need shoes," Kara said decisively. "Black is wrong for that dress. I've got some flats that are close to the blue color. You could borrow them if you like."

"There's a switch," Liz said dryly. "Kara lending something to Nancy. It's usually the other way around."

"Hey! Can I help it if Nancy's wardrobe is made to be raided?" Kara said, pretending to be wounded. She playfully tossed a sofa cushion at Liz's head, which Liz promptly tossed back.

"And I think my leather jacket will work better with your dress than yours will," said Dawn Steiger, a junior who was the Resident Advisor for the suite.

Nancy smiled gratefully at her. "Thanks," she

said. "Thanks to all of you for helping me out here. I really appreciate it."

"And now you guys have got to help me out," declared Eileen.

"*You* have a date?" Stephanie asked tactlessly, and Nancy noticed that Eileen blushed, although she said nothing. Nancy, along with most of the other women in the suite, knew that Eileen hadn't attracted any special male attention so far at college.

"Never mind," Eileen said awkwardly.

Nancy wondered what she had intended to say and wished Stephanie knew when to put a sock in her big mouth.

"Andy and I are going to the opening night with some of his friends," Reva put in to cover the uncomfortable silence. "Anyone else is welcome to go with us."

"Why not?" Ginny Yuen said. "Since Ray and his band are playing at the party afterward, he won't have much time for me. I'll go with you."

"Sounds good," said Liz.

Without looking at Stephanie, Eileen nodded. "Me, too."

"Fine," Stephanie said with a sigh. She stretched luxuriously. "Guess I wouldn't mind going with you, too. I mean, I had a couple of offers, but, well, you know."

Nancy smiled to herself. Stephanie never changed.

"What about you, Dawn?" Reva asked. "You've

been kind of grim and studious these last couple of weeks."

Nancy noticed that Dawn shifted uncomfortably. "Oh, I don't know," the R.A. said.

Nancy had been wondering about Dawn lately. She seemed lonely and withdrawn and hadn't joined in any campus activities. Nancy wasn't surprised when Dawn said she probably wouldn't be attending the party, and she found herself wishing that Dawn would find something to recharge her batteries.

"Well, I'd better hang this back up until its debut tomorrow," Nancy said, and headed back to her room. "I'm going to hit the showers before starting on my journalism assignment."

After putting away her dress, Nancy slipped into her bathrobe. Catching sight of herself in the mirrored closet door, Nancy muttered, "Another item on a shopping list when I get the time is a new bathrobe." Her favorite bathrobe had definitely seen better days. At one time it had been bright blue, but now it was faded and the shoulder seam had started unraveling. Still, who cared, she decided, gathering up her towel and shampoo. It was only her suitemates who saw her.

Just then there was a knock on the suite door. As she stepped out into the hall and started toward the bathroom, Nancy heard one of the women in the lounge jump up and open the door.

"Hey, everybody," a low male voice said.

"Hi, Jake." Stephanie's honeyed voice drifted back toward Nancy.

Jake! Nancy stopped and darted a look over her shoulder. Her eyes drank in his lean profile, his thick dark hair, and the way his red jacket set off the warm brown of his eyes. Her heart thudded wildly against her chest. And in the next second, she realized what she was wearing. Can you say nightmare?

"J-Jake," she almost squeaked, drawing her hand up to close the neck of her hopelessly disgusting bathrobe.

CHAPTER 2

Bess headed back from rehearsal to her dormitory, Jamison Hall. It was late, and she noticed that there were very few lights on in the old building. She let herself into the lobby and quietly took the stairs to her floor.

As she tiptoed into her room, Bess heard the sleeping, rhythmic breathing of her roommate, Leslie King. How can anyone sleep? she wondered. Bess's head was still reeling with the sights and sounds of the rehearsal, the music echoing in her ears. Thank goodness for Brian and his boring video, she thought. I'm going to need it after all.

After changing into her bathrobe, Bess wandered out into the floor's lounge. She slipped the video into the VCR and settled back on the sofa, preparing herself for a yawnathon of extraterrestrial creatures on intergalactic battlegrounds. She was surprised to see instead the interior of Java Joe's, Wilder University's popular coffeehouse. The camera panned slowly down the aisles, taking in students talking and sipping from Java Joe's trademark brown mugs, then zoomed in on a back booth and moved in for a close-up of Brian sitting with Chris Vogel, the production assistant from the play.

Bess sighed. Brian must have accidentally given her the wrong tape. She halfheartedly watched the scene before her. Why would anyone bother to tape a couple of friends sitting at a coffeehouse? Talk about pointless. Suddenly Bess scooted up to the edge of the sofa and frowned. She couldn't quite put a finger on what she was feeling, but ... yes, there it was.

Chris and Brian were laughing and exchanging confidences. There was a look between the two. The unmistakable current between two people who are more than friends. Bess had known for some time that Brian was gay, but he had made her promise not to tell anyone because he wasn't ready to go public about his homosexuality. Yet, here it was on tape. She realized anyone watching the video would draw the conclusion that Brian and Chris were closer than friends. Bess was startled when an electronically altered voice crackled as the tape continued to play: "Smile—you're on 'Candid Camera.' And a copy of this touching scene will be sent to your esteemed parents unless you send a nice little sum—say five hundred dollars—to me immediately. A little—shall we call it—*hush* money."

Bess froze. Someone was threatening to tell all about Brian. He was being blackmailed!

"I brought your reporter's notebook. You left it on your desk, and I thought you might need it," Jake said quickly as his eyes swept over Nancy. He blinked as he took in her bathrobe and obvious embarrassment. Great timing, Collins. "You didn't have to get all dressed up for me," he attempted to joke.

Nancy turned several shades of red and looked to Jake as though she wanted to run and hide. Then she seemed to recover her cool, as she tossed back her reddish blond hair and grinned. "Oh, you mean this ol' thing?" she said, smiling.

Jake laughed. He had to hand it to Nancy— she had a great sense of humor. "Well, anyway, I saw your notebook, and I was just passing by and—" Jake stopped, and in spite of himself, his eyes made their way down her legs. They were incredibly long and shapely. He willed himself to look back up to her face but found he was watching her gracefully sloping neck. Wow, he thought, Nancy is a knockout—even in an old bathrobe. Okay, so try to keep this meeting professional, Collins.

He heard himself speaking in a rush. "I was talking to Gail about that article you were interested in doing for the features section, and she thought it was a good idea, but that maybe it needed more developing. Since she is the editor-in-chief, I couldn't exactly disagree with her, although I thought your idea was interesting."

Abruptly, Jake realized that as he and Nancy were talking, the eyes of at least four other attractive young women were on him. He turned and smiled shyly at Nancy's suitemates, feeling awkward but still enjoying all the female attention. But he didn't want Nancy to be any more embarrassed than she already was.

"Well, I'd better get a move on. Here's your notebook," he said, handing it to her. "See you later."

" 'Bye," Nancy said, and gave him the full treatment with her cool blue eyes.

Well, you kept it professional, Collins, but that woman sure does something to you, Jake thought to himself as he hurried out and down the stairs. Once outside, Jake took in a deep lungful of the cool night air. He couldn't wait until the following evening. He imagined sitting next to Nancy in the darkened theater, and then afterward at the party, holding her close in his arms as they danced. In his mind, they were the only two at the party.

Back in his dorm room, Brian lay sleeplessly on top of his Hudson Bay blanket. What was the use? he asked himself, stretching up to snap on his halogen study lamp. He reached into his back-pack for a book, but his hand encountered the smooth surface of a videotape. Furrowing his brow, he pulled it out. *Release from Planet Zero,* he read. What?

"No, no, no," he moaned as the realization dawned on him. He'd given Bess the wrong tape! He had to stop her from watching it. No one must know what was happening. No one.

Maybe, he thought, jumping up and pulling on his clothes, he'd get lucky. Bess might not have watched it yet. He'd just explain that there was a mix-up, that he'd accidentally given her the wrong thing and swap tapes with her.

Brian bolted out into the night and raced toward Jamison Hall. Minutes later he groaned in frustration as he tried the locked door. Before he had time to consider how he'd get into the building, someone opened the door and stepped out into the night. Brian slipped in before the door sprang shut again, then flew up the stairs two at a time. He knocked on the lounge door, hoping Bess was still up and nearby to hear him. He exhaled in relief as Bess opened it. Behind her, Brian could see the bluish haze of the TV screen as he entered the darkened room.

"Bess!" he said, then froze as he saw the scene playing on the TV.

Bess looked up at him, her blue eyes questioning. "Brian, tell me what's going on," she said quietly, clicking the remote and moving over to remove the tape from the VCR.

"Nothing," Brian said. He reached for the tape. "You weren't supposed to see that. I just messed up. I brought you *Release from Planet Zero*. Here."

But Bess held on to the tape. "Brian, there *is* something going on," she said, sitting down on the sofa. "And I think you'd better clue me in as to what it is."

Brian searched her face for a moment, then his shoulders sagged and he collapsed onto the sofa next to her, putting down the tape he'd brought and dropping his head into his hands. He was silent for a few moments, then raised his head and spoke.

"It's pretty simple," he said. "Someone is threatening to tell my parents that I'm gay. I guess whoever it was saw me and Chris together, and, well . . . you saw the tape. It came in the mail the other day." Brian sighed, and Bess touched his hand. He attempted a smile at her concern and continued talking.

"I've gotten other notes and things. Whoever it is wants money. Lots of it. So, I've been paying. I mail payments to a P.O. box in Weston. I sent one just yesterday, for that." Brian pointed to the tape in Bess's hands.

Bess shook her head. "That's awful," she raged. "Whether or not you tell your parents about your lifestyle is no one's business. No one has the right to force you to speak up if you don't want to."

"I guess someone sees it as a business opportunity." Brian laughed hollowly. "They see it as a way to make money—a lot of money."

"Well, if you tell your parents yourself, then whoever this creep is will just have to find another way to earn money,'" Bess replied.

Brian got up, walked over to the window, and looked out at the campus. There were a few lights on, but it seemed as if almost everyone was sleeping. He wondered if the person who was blackmailing him was sleeping. Groaning, he turned back to Bess.

"It's not that easy," he said, running his hand through his tousled blond hair. "I don't need to tell you that my parents probably wouldn't understand." He laughed hollowly. "Call that the understatement of the century. 'A-hem, Mr. Councilman, I understand your son is gay.' Imagine the voters getting hold of that piece of news."

"What are you talking about?" Bess asked.

"My dad is a councilman in my hometown— it's a pretty big suburb of Milwaukee," Brian explained. "It also happens to be your basic conservative district. Thing is, my dad's reelection is getting closer, and from what my mom tells me and the things I've been reading in my hometown paper, the election's neck-and-neck. Something like this would tip the scales in favor of my dad's opponent. And my blackmailer seems to be banking on it."

"Do you have an enemy that you know of? Who could be doing this to you?" Bess asked.

Brian shook his head. "I have absolutely no idea. None."

"Well, you can't let this jerk get away with it!" Bess declared. "Let's tell Nancy. She can't stand seeing anyone in trouble. I'll bet she could help you—somehow."

Brian turned toward Bess, real alarm in his eyes. "No," he said flatly. "You've got to promise me you won't tell anyone. No one else can know."

"But you've got to get help. What's to keep the blackmailer from telling everything after bleeding you out of a ton of money?"

Brian turned to face the window. "I'll just have to figure this out on my own. I can't tell a soul. If it leaked out by accident . . ." He shuddered. "Not even Chris knows."

"Chris doesn't know?" Bess asked. "But he's part of this mess."

Brian turned to her sadly. "I just didn't want to drag anyone else into it."

"Well, I still think we should enlist Nancy's help," Bess said. As she spoke, Brian heard the sympathy and love in her voice, and felt grateful for her friendship.

"But if you're not going to tell anyone," Bess continued, "at least you've got to warn Chris." Brian snapped to attention.

"After all," Bess said, meeting Brian's gaze, "he

cares about you very much, and this affects him, too. You have to tell him, Brian—tomorrow!"

"That was so nice of you to get all these snacks for the party," Casey said to Eileen early the next morning as the two young women walked together to the Kappa house, hoisting several grocery bags. "I've just been so busy with rehearsals and all. Thanks so much."

Eileen took note of Casey's million megawatt grin as she shifted one of the heavy bags, and she gave the lovely redhead beside her a brief nod. No wonder Casey had been the lead on one of TV's hottest sitcoms, *The President's Daughter.* That million megawatt smile.

"Oh, you're welcome," Eileen said with a warmth she didn't feel.

Ordinarily, it wouldn't have been a big deal to make a quick stop at the local mini-mart that Wilder students frequented. But, Eileen thought darkly, she was busy herself, with two papers due and all the pledge activities she'd had to fit in during the last couple of weeks. Why couldn't Miss Gorgeous figure out how to deal with all the extra sorority demands? Still, she wasn't about to get into a hassle with Kappa's most famous pledge, the legendary Casey Fontaine, teen star. It just wasn't worth it. It had been easier to agree to pick up the bags of chips and pretzels and other goodies that would be served at the party.

At least Casey had taken the trouble to help her carry them from the dorm to the sorority house.

"You know," Casey went on, talking in her light, lilting voice. "I love being at Wilder. People in Hollywood thought I was crazy when I quit the show to go to school. But I made the right decision. Everyone here is great. You and the cast from *Grease!* and of course all the women in Kappa. I'm flattered that they let me pledge so late and all."

Eileen forced a smile and thought back to some of the students' comments during the discussion that Melina Stavros's political science class had had at the Student Union. She wondered what Casey would think if she knew what some people around Wilder really were thinking.

"Well, just be glad you didn't have to go through early pledging," she said. "I mean, you saw for yourself how humiliating it was. Wearing books on your head, bursting into the Kappa anthem no matter where you were. Doing things you'd never dream of doing, hoping you'd meet with the approval of people you hardly knew."

Casey's eyes were wide. "Sounds like auditions. In the entertainment business, they're referred to as cattle calls. That's exactly what I felt like on some auditions—one of the cattle," she said softly.

Eileen looked at Casey. It never occurred to her that actresses felt like that. She'd just assumed that anyone who went to an audition never gave it a second thought. "Actually, things were worse those first few days of pledging. I mean, some of the upperclassmen treated us like servants," Eileen confessed, suddenly feeling that she could open up to Casey, now that Casey had shared a sort of private thought.

"That surprises me," Casey said. "Everyone's been so nice to me."

Eileen felt her annoyance returning. She doubted everyone would be "so nice" if Casey weren't a big star. She thought about how coolly Soozie Beckerman, Kappa's secretary, treated her and the rest of the pledges. Yet Soozie had nearly drooled all over Casey when Casey first showed up at Kappa.

The two young women entered the kitchen and set the bags on the counter next to Soozie. Eileen noticed that Casey made no move to put away the contents of the bags. She just waved hello to Soozie and followed the Kappa secretary toward the living room, as if expecting Eileen to take care of the groceries. Well, Eileen decided on the spot, she wouldn't. She walked into the living room, too. Let someone else do the honors of putting away the food. She wasn't going to be pushed around.

"There you are." Soozie's voice dripped disapproval as Eileen walked into the light, airy room. Eileen noticed that many of the other pledges were there, as well as a number of upper-class sorority sisters. Soozie called out, "Holly, Casey and Eileen are here."

Eileen felt a lump go to her throat. What was wrong? Had the pledges done something wrong? Why was Holly Thornton, the sorority president, looking for them? True, Holly was always watching out for the pledges, but Soozie never let up for an instant. She would go for blood if given half a chance. And if anything were to go wrong with Kappa's all-important party plans, Eileen knew they'd never hear the end of it.

"Sit down, guys," Holly said, walking directly over to Casey.

"What's up?" Casey asked, darting a questioning glance at Eileen, who shrugged.

"Bad news," Soozie said, frowning.

"Someone's complained to the campus chapter of the Panhellenic Council," Holly said.

"What's that?" Casey asked, wide-eyed.

"They're a governing organization that decides rush rules for sororities all over the country," Soozie said.

"So?" Casey asked, prompting her.

Get on with it. Tell us what's going on, Eileen wanted to scream.

"Turns out someone wasn't happy that we allowed Casey to pledge without going through all the official rush procedures," Holly said soberly. "Now the Panhellenic Council is launching an investigation."

"Putting it simply, Kappa could be in big trouble," Soozie said, her eyes narrowing.

CHAPTER 3

"Hey, where is everybody?" Bess said as she entered Kappa's kitchen and set down the large box of old-fashioned straw dispensers she'd rented for the party. Oh, they look perfect, she thought to herself. She was disappointed that no one was there, because she was just bursting to talk about the party. She'd spent all morning holed up in a class and then the library, and she was aching to chat about something fun for a change.

"Massive goodies!" she said, looking with satisfaction at the jumbled boxes and bags on the counters. Mountains of cookies, potato chip, and pretzel bags sat on the counter with hot dog and hamburger buns. Bess felt her mouth water. It had been hours since she'd had breakfast, and she stared hungrily at the sealed food bags. She heard Holly call as she was about to open the refrigerator.

"Bess, in here." Holly's voice came from the living room. Bess grabbed a couple of carrot sticks from one of the platefuls of cut-up vegetables. She swirled them in a bowl of ranch dip, crunching as she made her way to the living room.

Everything looks ready, she was about to say to the group of Kappa women sitting on the sofas and gathered by the fireplace. But noticing the serious expressions of Holly, Eileen, and Casey, Bess stopped in midcrunch. Why did everyone look so somber? Holly and Soozie had Casey cornered by the fireplace, and from the look on Casey's face, Bess could plainly see something was wrong. Maybe the pledges forgot something, Bess thought in horror. But what could it be? The place was perfectly decorated.

"What is it?" she asked, glancing at Holly.

Holly's face was set, her jaw tense, as she said, "I've just been explaining to Casey that someone went to the Panhellenic Council and registered a formal complaint because Kappa allowed Casey to pledge without going through the rush procedures."

"You're kidding!" Bess exploded.

Casey nodded miserably. "Whoever it was felt pretty strongly, I guess, or she wouldn't have gone to so much trouble."

"But that's ridiculous. That's no one's business

but Kappa's," Bess sputtered. "Anyway, what can they do?"

"Plenty," Soozie said, her eyes slipping over Bess in a way that always left Bess feeling she didn't quite measure up. Instinctively, Bess looked down to see if she'd spilled a glob of ranch dip on her tights or something.

"They happen to be the governing board for sororities all over the country," Soozie went on. "If they want to make a big deal about the fact that we bent the rules, well, they can."

"No one bent any rules," Bess started to say. "Well, maybe tweaked them a little."

Casey shook her head. "No," she said. *"Broken* probably is the word. I hate bringing trouble to Kappa." She looked around the room.

"You didn't bring on any trouble," Soozie said. "Whoever lodged the complaint brought on the trouble. You're not the problem at all. You're our best asset."

Bess noticed that Casey colored a little. Bess guessed that it made her uncomfortable to be discussed as if she were a commodity.

"What are we going to do?" Bess asked her sisters.

"We'll just straighten out Panhellenic," declared one of them.

Soozie snorted.

Casey stood up. "I can't deal with this. I mean, you guys are my friends. I hate causing you problems. I'm going to resign. That should take care of it."

"No way!" Bess exclaimed.

"No," Holly said. "We'll think of something."

Casey looked uncertainly at them. "Well, I just don't want the sorority to get into trouble on account of me."

Holly put an arm around Casey. "We'll work something out. I've dealt with Panhellenic before. And we're not going to worry about it now. We'll get through the party and the play, then we'll have a meeting and bump heads as to what to do. Don't even think of resigning."

"Well, thanks," Casey said.

Bess crumpled onto the arm of the nearest sofa and tried to collect her thoughts. There was too much to handle at once. The play, the party, Brian's situation, and now this! When were things going to start easing up? She wasn't sure how much stress she could take. Already her face had broken out, and she was only hours away from stepping on stage.

A couple of the girls, including Casey, got up and left the room, but Bess didn't budge. She sat moodily staring out the bay window onto the tree-lined street.

"So, Bess . . ." Soozie's voice drifted into her reality. "Speaking of the play, how's rehearsal going for you and your *friend* Brian?"

Bess blinked. There was something in the way Soozie was looking at her that Bess couldn't quite read, but it was more than the usual disapproval Soozie seemed to reserve for her. More than once Bess had wondered if Soozie had guessed Brian's secret. Still, Soozie was a Kappa, and she was a pledge, and Bess knew she'd better pretend she didn't notice the icy way Soozie treated her.

"Oh, just fine," she answered brightly. "Dress rehearsal went really well. Brian's part is small, but he's the only freshman guy with a speaking role. I'm absolutely certain he's going to knock 'em dead."

Soozie's eyes penetrated Bess. "Brian's such a natural for the theater profession, don't you think? I mean, he's so good at pretending."

With that she flounced out of the room. Bess watched her retreating back. A chilling thought pushed its way to the front of her brain. Was Soozie the one blackmailing Brian? She shook her head as if to rid herself of the thought. That was the last thing she needed. If Bess made an accusation she couldn't back up, Soozie wouldn't hesitate for a second to put an end to her career as a pledge. And Bess didn't want to risk that. Being accepted by a group of fellow arts lovers like the Kappas meant too much to her. She'd felt adrift when she first came to Wilder, until she'd been accepted as a pledge at Kappa. She couldn't let anything ruin the family feeling she was experiencing with her Kappa sisters.

But then, Bess thought, no one deserved to be blackmailed the way Brian was, either. And

Brian was also her friend. Friends were supposed to help each other, weren't they? Bess made up her mind. She'd watch Soozie, to see what she could find out. She'd just have to be extra careful. And if Soozie was the blackmailer, Bess would catch her.

A noisy group of drama students burst out the front door of the Hewlitt theater complex. They spilled down the stairway and moved in great waves, fanning out in all directions on the ivy-covered Wilder campus. Brian glanced back at Chris, who was lagging behind, talking with one of the drama professors.

Brian watched Chris closely and noticed how animated he was. His dark head gleamed in the late Friday afternoon sun and he threw his head back as he laughed. That was one thing Brian liked about Chris—he was always so lighthearted and carefree. It was easy to coax a laugh from him. *If only I didn't have to tell him about this,* he thought darkly. *He doesn't need to be troubled right now.* Still, Bess was right. Chris had a right to know what was going on. He walked slowly ahead toward the academic quad while Chris finished his conversation.

"Hey, wait up," Chris called a couple of seconds later. He rushed up behind Brian, brushing his leather-jacketed sleeve. Brian hunched his shoulders and walked on, looking at him sideways.

"Something wrong?" Chris asked, worry blowing across his face like a storm cloud.

Brian ached to just keep walking and assuring him that nothing was wrong. But Bess was right. Chris was affected in a big way. Brian slowed just a bit.

"No. Well, yeah," he said in a low voice. "Not a big deal, exactly. But there's something you should know. You don't know how much I hate telling you this."

Chris's face drained of its color. "You don't want to see me anymore."

Brian made sure no one was within listening distance. "No, that's not it at all," he said. "But I might as well just lay it out. Someone knows about us."

The relief on Chris's face was unmistakable. "Oh, is that all."

"I wish it were," Brian went on. "Keep walking. We don't want to be overheard. The thing is, this person, I don't know who it is, is banking on the fact that I don't want anyone to know about my lifestyle. I'm being blackmailed, Chris."

"What?" Chris stopped in the middle of the Walk.

Brian explained briefly about the increasingly threatening notes he'd been receiving. He told Chris about paying out large sums of money so that the blackmailer wouldn't tell his parents about their relationship. He explained what it would do to his dad's career if word were to get out. Without waiting for Chris to comment, Brian finished up by telling him about the tape he'd accidentally given to Bess.

"She was the one who made me promise to tell you. She said you had a right to know since you were mixed up in this."

Chris shrugged and ran his hand through his jet black hair. "There is such a thing as a right to privacy," he said calmly. "Let's take it to the campus authorities. No reason you and I should be prey to jerks like this."

Brian put up his hand. "No," he said flatly. "We can't tell anyone. If word got back to my hometown, it could ruin my dad's reelection."

Chris opened his mouth to protest but then shut it again. "Fine," he said simply. "We'll figure out something." Then changing the subject abruptly, he added, "By the way, Professor Farber said that this year's freshmen actors are the most promising talent he's had at Wilder in years. He mentioned that if you keep it up, you're sure to have some major parts in the next couple of years."

Brian felt warmed by the secondhand praise, his worries momentarily forgotten. Praise from Professor Farber was rare.

"He said that?" Brian exclaimed. "Well, that's good news at least, and I sure need some. I'm so nervous about tonight, I feel sick. It was all I could do to get through classes today."

Chris reached into his backpack. "I know

you're going to do great. But just in case you need some extra luck, I got you an opening night gift."

He pulled out a small green box, which he handed to Brian. Brian felt his face heat up with pleasure, and he gave Chris a warm smile.

"Thanks a lot, man," he said, suddenly feeling shy. "I'll open it just before the show."

"It's also a thank-you for being such a good friend," Chris said directly to him. Then he glanced at his watch. "I'm late for class. Got to run. I'll see you at the play tonight." With that, he gave Brian's shoulder a quick squeeze and took off.

Brian stood on the walk and turned the box over and over in his hands, feeling better than he had for days. Chris hadn't seemed fazed by the news. Well, maybe things would work out, Brian decided as he started to head back to the theater complex. He certainly hoped so. He couldn't afford to blast his dad's political career. It meant everything to him, and his dad would never forgive him if he were the reason his career was derailed.

Well, isn't that touching? A sweet gift exchange. From a window on the third floor of the academic quad, a camera was trained on Brian and Chris on the walk below. *Whirr, click, click.* The telephoto lens was strong, capturing every detail, right up to the expressions on the two guys' faces.

Quickly, now hurry. These magic moments are so fleeting. And, someone's bound to come into this lecture hall soon. You don't want to be caught just when the money's rolling in, do you?

What a lucky break. This was merely supposed to be a place to slip in and think about my next move. How lucky that Chris and Brian happened along just now. And how fortunate to have a camera at the right time to record an unmistakable encounter. Now a quick trip to the one-hour photo place. This is the perfect opportunity for another request for money. A bigger request— just in time for opening night.

The note accompanying the photos will be something like: Have recorded another touching moment between you and Chris that I'm sure you'll want to share with the world. Or maybe not? Then make the usual payment. But this time, double it. Pay up in the usual way, et cetera, et cetera. Something close to that but short and to the point. Brian will get the message.

Oh, today's work was good. When Brian sees this, he'll realize that he isn't the only one with talent.

CHAPTER 4

Jake's here," Kara said, bounding into the room she shared with Nancy. "Well, almost here. I saw him walking toward Thayer while I was in the lobby."

Nancy looked up from the mirror where she was fastening the necklace that Reva had lent her.

"Great," she said simply, with a calm she didn't feel. Even now, her hand was shaking as she tried to do up the clasp on the black cord. Jake's here, Jake's here—the words echoed through her brain. Nancy studied her face in the mirror. Ordinarily, she didn't make such a big deal about how she looked, but tonight was special. Jake was special.

"Let me help you, O She of the Unsteady Hand," Kara said. She shook her head and laughed as she fastened Nancy's clasp. "There. You have nothing to be nervous about. You look great. Jake is going to absolutely lose it when he sees you."

"What are you going to wear?" Nancy asked, standing back and taking note of Kara's tousled hair and baggy Wilder sweats.

"Well, just when I thought I'd borrowed everything worth wearing in your closet, I found this," Kara said, pulling out a long, black skirt from under a heap of clothes on her bed. "And I was sure I had a blouse somewhere, too. Oh, here it is. Now, where are those hair combs I borrowed from Ginny?"

Nancy smiled in amusement as Hurricane Kara whirled into action. Setting a land-speed record in getting dressed, Kara was transformed into a stylish supervixen, ready to take on the night.

"You look unbelievable," Nancy said sincerely.

"Thanks," Kara said. She did a dip and a swirl in her borrowed finery. "I hope Tim thinks so, too."

"Tim's completely recovered, hasn't he?" Nancy asked, knowing how concerned Kara had been about Tim Downing's close call with hypothermia. Kara and Tim were dating when he'd been hurt in the Alpha hazing incident, and she had stood vigil over Tim while he was in the hospital.

Kara nodded. "His doctors still want him to take it easy. His body went through a terrible shock. It's my job to make sure his body's well taken care of."

She grinned wickedly, and Nancy laughed. "Kara!" she protested at her roommate's outrageousness.

Just then Jake appeared in the doorway. Nancy's breath momentarily caught in her throat as she gazed shyly into Jake's beautiful eyes. Talk about cute! Jake's wavy brown hair fell across his forehead in a sexy way. In keeping with the *Grease!* theme, he was wearing a white T-shirt with a black leather bomber jacket tossed casually over it. He looked tall and slender in his close-fitting jeans. Of course, Nancy noted, he was wearing his signature black, silver-tipped cowboy boots.

"Hi," she said, hoping her voice didn't betray the range of emotions she was feeling.

"Hi yourself," Jake said, his eyes sweeping down her. "You look unbelievably beautiful."

Nancy shivered. "Thank you," she said, taking a deep breath.

"See you there," Kara said, heading out to join her friends in the lounge.

"Okay." Nancy picked up the jacket Dawn had lent her and walked toward Jake. He reached over to help her with her jacket. "All set?" he asked, his hand lingering on her shoulders a little longer than necessary.

Nancy nodded. "All set."

As they walked toward the Hewlitt theater

complex, Nancy automatically looked over at the building where the *Wilder Times* was housed. She saw that Jake had done the same thing.

"Caught you," they said to each other at the same time, and laughed.

"We have to promise each other not to bring up the newspaper or journalism tonight," Jake said.

Nancy nodded. "It's a deal," she agreed. "Time out tonight. I don't want to see you whip out your reporter's notebook even once. We're here to watch a play, not report on it."

"Good. We've got that settled," Jake said. He took her hand, and Nancy shivered as she felt the warmth of his hand. This was why she was here at Wilder, she decided—to feel this explosively happy.

"But," Jake continued, "if we're not going to talk about the paper, we have to talk about something else. And I want to know more about you."

Nancy found herself slowing down to keep pace with Jake's relaxed but purposeful walk. "Okay," she said, turning to face him. "What do you want to know?"

Jake's brown eyes bored into hers as he said simply, "Everything."

Nancy found that it was amazingly right to tell him all kinds of things. About her father, internationally known lawyer Carson Drew and his new girlfriend, Avery Fallon. It seemed natural to explain how happy it made her to see her father really content after all the years he'd spent as a widower. Then she touched on her breakup with her longtime boyfriend, Ned Nickerson.

"It was really hard saying goodbye to Ned," she confessed. "But I knew that I couldn't go and exist as his shadow at Emerson College. I had to move on and find out more about the world. None of it was easy."

"It's never easy saying goodbye to someone you love," Jake said mysteriously, and Nancy wondered if there was a story behind his words. Maybe she was on her way to finding out more about him.

When Nancy asked Jake about himself, however, Jake turned the questions back to her. As he probed gently, she found herself talking even more about herself. Jake already knew what had happened between her and Peter Goodwin, but it felt good to let him know that she no longer was hurt by it. Jake listened actively, asking her a few questions here and there without seeming to pry.

She found it easy to tell Jake that even though she'd decided not to let anything distract her from immersing herself in university life, she hadn't been too successful when her friends were in trouble. She told him about some of the mysteries she'd solved since arriving at Wilder.

"How do you get involved in these things?" Jake asked, after hearing about Nancy's most recent exploits.

Nancy shrugged. "Well, I think I get mixed up in things because I want to help my friends," she confessed.

Before starting up the stairs of the Hewlitt theater complex, Jake pulled Nancy out of the stream of people making their way into the theater. He stopped and took her face between his hands. "Well, this time you've got your work cut out for you. The biggest unsolved mystery of all time could be our relationship."

Nancy smiled, feeling emotions tumble through her. Jake pulled his hands away and they walked on. Saying nothing as they continued through the theater doors, Nancy found herself hoping that it didn't take long to unravel this particular mystery.

George Fayne and Will Blackfeather made their way through the crowd milling around the backstage door.

"We've got to see Bess before she goes onstage," George said. "I promised her. She was suffering from a lethal dose of stage fright this afternoon."

"This way," Will said, fast-talking his way in past the security guard and pulling George in with him. "Though I hate to disappoint you, we may never find her in this mess."

"There she is," George called triumphantly, spying Bess and Casey standing in a crush of people by the light panels at stage left. She maneuvered her way over.

"George, you're here," Bess cried, reaching up to bear-hug her cousin. "Hi, Will. Well, this is it—make it or break it time."

"I think you'll be a hit," Will said.

George said hello to Casey, and thought the actress seemed cool and professional as she accepted everyone's good wishes. Of course, a school play was nothing compared to her television experience. Still, on closer inspection, George realized Casey looked every bit as nervous as her fellow actors.

As the talk swirled around her, George glanced toward Brian, who was standing next to Bess. He seemed anything but cool. His jaw was tense and George could see that he was terribly uneasy. Talk about stage fright.

Looking past Brian, George saw Nancy and Jake making their way up to the group from the direction of the auditorium. Nancy's face was lit with an inner glow, and there was no mistaking the sparks flying between the two. George reached for Will's hand and studied Nancy and Jake as they hugged Bess and Casey and wished them luck. It looks as if Nancy has a great thing going, she thought. After a while Will drifted over to speak with someone he knew, and George felt someone tugging on her sleeve.

"Come with me while I finish putting on my

makeup," Bess begged, her face drawn and pale under the garish overhead lights.

"Okay," George agreed, knowing how nervous Bess must be feeling.

Bess had set up her stuff in the corner of the cramped and crowded chorus dressing room. As Bess applied eye shadow, George kept up a steady stream of small talk to try to calm her. George commented on the tiny size of the dressing room and the lighting, chatted about how beautiful Nancy looked tonight—anything but the fact that the curtain would be rising in a short while. While she talked, George marveled at how a dressing area so small could hold so many laughing and chattering actresses, all milling around, borrowing one another's curling irons and zipping each other into bright, shiny costumes.

"So, George," Bess interrupted suddenly, "have you ever betrayed a confidence to help someone you cared about?"

"Huh?" George was taken by surprise. Bess was about to step onstage for her opening night, and here she was talking about something that made no sense.

"Have you?" Bess persisted.

George frowned. "No. If someone told me to keep my mouth shut, I'd do it. It's that simple. But what does this have to do with anything here?"

Bess shrugged, making a face into the mirror

as she reapplied mascara and lipstick. "Just wondered," she said.

"I don't think you should ever go behind a friend's back," George added, wondering what Bess was really trying to say. But just then the assistant director poked her head into the dressing room. "Cast members, places everyone." The woman's glance fell on George. "I'm sorry, but the play is about to begin. You'll have to leave."

"I wish you didn't have to go, George," Bess said desperately. "I need you."

George squeezed her cousin's shoulder. "I'd stay, but that dragon lady looks like she'd shred me if I did. Will and I would be front row center, but we could only afford cheaper seats. Don't worry, though, we'll applaud the loudest. You're gonna be great. Break a leg and all that."

"Oh," Bess moaned. "Who was the sickie who came up with a phrase as ominous as 'break a leg' anyway?"

After George left, Bess put the finishing touches on her makeup and checked her hair. She stood up and smoothed her fifties costume, giving herself a last once-over in the mirror before leaving the crowded dressing room. This is it, she said to herself as she walked toward the wings where the rest of the chorus was congregating.

It was dark in the wings, and Bess could hear the university orchestra start up the high-spirited strains of the overture. She closed her eyes and prayed fervently that she would remember all her steps and not bring supreme humiliation upon herself.

Suddenly a camera flash flooded the area with light, causing some chorus members to protest. Bess's eyes blinked rapidly as she was momentarily blinded, but when her eyes adjusted, she caught sight of Erik Grenquist lowering his camera. Following his gaze, Bess saw that he was staring intently at Brian.

A crazy thought popped into her mind then. Could it be Erik who was blackmailing Brian? Bess watched as the skinny freshman slipped away into the darkened area backstage. After all, he had practically ripped off Brian's head when Brian accidentally brushed against him at rehearsal the other day. The look Erik had given Brian was one of pure loathing. She barely knew him, but he seemed like the type of guy who could hold a grudge—and maybe even stoop to blackmail. No, the idea was too obvious, too easy.

Bess studied Brian, who was nervously waiting for his cue. Poor Brian, she thought. He doesn't need this on top of everything. If only she could figure out who the blackmailer was, who was making Brian's life so miserable. But just then thoughts of blackmailers were swept away as she heard her cue. It was show time! Bess took a deep breath and stepped onto the stage, where the audience awaited.

*   *   *

The curtain fell as Nancy and Jake jumped to their feet and joined in the resounding applause around them.

"Weren't they spectacular?" Jake exclaimed enthusiastically.

"Way to kick butt!" someone shouted.

"That's not how I'd put it maybe, but they were incredible," Nancy shouted over the din of shrill whistles and cheers. "Wilder will be talking about this production for years."

She watched the stage when the curtain went up again and redoubled her applause as Bess, Brian, Casey, and the rest of the chorus stepped up for their bow. It was clear to Nancy at that moment that Bess was in her element. Her curvy frame was practically wriggling from excitement, and her smile lit up the entire theater complex. George leaned over and hugged Nancy.

"Bess did it," she yelled exultantly. "They all did it! I'm so proud."

"We all are," Nancy said, her eyes shining. While the orchestra played one more reprise of *Grease!* she looked over at Jake and studied his profile. A calm happiness stole over her as she followed Jake onto the stage to congratulate their friends.

When they got backstage, Nancy joined in the happy throng surrounding the cast. "You were wonderful!" she exclaimed, hugging Bess.

"We did it!" Bess said over and over again, her blue eyes sparkling more than ever. She and

Casey and Brian and Chris put their arms around one another, jumping up and down, laughing and hugging.

"Great job, man," Jake said to Brian.

"He was the best," Bess agreed.

But instead of smiling at the praise as Nancy expected him to, Brian's body suddenly went rigid and his face became expressionless. She turned and saw that his eyes had locked onto an older, well-dressed couple standing near them. The man, wearing an expensive tailored suit, was an older version of Brian—same classic good looks, though with a few more laugh lines, and silvery streaks through his thick blond hair. The woman had the long, regal neck of a fashion model, and her hair was swept back in an elegant style. Her eyes were the same beautiful green as Brian's. She was smiling at Brian, but he wasn't returning the smile.

"Why are you here? I thought you couldn't make it," Brian said flatly as they approached.

Nancy blinked at the harsh words and stared at the couple, then back at Brian. If these were Brian's parents, he sure had a strange way of welcoming them.

"We couldn't miss your first university production." The man's deep, rich voice carried over the noise. He shifted slightly and cleared his throat a few times. Clearly, he was nervous, Nancy observed.

"We're, um, Brian's parents," the woman said,

her cheeks growing pink with embarrassment when Brian didn't introduce them. "I'm Marjorie, and this is Bob."

"Bob Daglian," Mr. Daglian said heartily, reaching over to shake hands in a practiced way with Jake and Nancy.

"You could have called," Brian said, still regarding his parents coldly.

"Brian . . ." Chris said, under his breath.

"Oh, we changed our plans at the last minute so we could see you perform," Brian's mother chattered brightly. "We thought we'd make you nervous by telling you beforehand. We didn't think you would mind if we just showed up."

"Well, I do mind," Brian stated.

"Brian," his mother said in a shocked voice. "What's gotten into you? We thought you'd be glad to see us."

Nancy didn't get it. Brian had always seemed to be so nice. He ought to be happy that his parents had gone to such trouble to see him perform. Why was he treating them this way and making a scene?

"Next time, save the trip," Brian snapped, then turned and took off, leaving everyone standing around awkwardly.

Something's definitely going on here, Nancy thought. She glanced at Bess. And Bess knows what it is!

CHAPTER 5

"Brian, wait!" Bess shouted, and took off after him. Nancy stood rooted in confusion, then glanced around her at the shocked faces. She locked eyes with Mrs. Daglian and noticed how hard the older woman was trying to hide her hurt. She was smiling bravely, and Nancy's heart went out to her. Imagine your own son acting as though he wished you'd never shown up, Nancy thought.

"Well, that's Brian for you," Mr. Daglian said smoothly to fill the awkward moment. "Too modest to stay around long enough for the accolades."

"Which is too bad because he certainly deserves them for his wonderful performance," said Casey, without missing a beat. "He really helped me out of a jam at the end of the first act. I was about to turn the wrong way, and Brian guided me so no one would notice. I could have ended up crashing into the rest of the chorus. Well, anyway, if you'll excuse me, I've got to get this makeup off."

That was incredibly nice of her, Nancy thought. Casey found something to praise in someone else's performance.

"Wasn't that the young woman from *The President's Daughter?*" Mrs. Daglian asked.

Nancy assured her that it was, glad for a topic to keep the conversation rolling. Jake and Chris deftly picked up the threads. Nancy watched as Mr. and Mrs. Daglian responded graciously. They were amazingly calm, considering what had just happened. No wonder they were such a success in political circles. They were obviously used to warming up crowds.

While Brian's parents were charming his friends, Nancy peered worriedly in the direction where Brian and Bess had disappeared. What on earth was going on? But she hid her confusion and concern and returned to the conversation buzzing around her.

As the crowds started thinning out backstage, Brian returned, followed by Bess. He was obviously embarrassed, his cheeks flushed and showing even under his makeup.

"I'm sorry, everyone," he said sheepishly. "I didn't introduce you properly to my parents."

"That's all right," Jake said. "No introductions

necessary. We've just been getting to know one another."

Nancy looked at Jake gratefully, and soon Brian moved a little way off to talk with his parents. She wondered what Bess had said to make him come back.

"Well, we're off," George said as Will put an arm around her. "It's time to party."

"See you there," Nancy said. She knew George and Will would rather be alone than show up at a party, but Nancy also knew that George would never miss her cousin's big night.

Just then Nancy spotted Gail Gardeski, editor-in-chief of the *Wilder Times*. She debated about saying hello to her. Gail intimidated her because she always made Nancy feel like the most novice cub reporter. Oh, come on, Nancy chided herself, striding over to where Gail was standing. Unfortunately, Gail was involved in a deep discussion with the director of *Grease!* and didn't notice her. Finally, not wanting to interrupt Gail, Nancy moved back over to her own group.

Seconds later Gail looked up and saw Nancy and Jake. She waved at Nancy but motioned Jake to come over to meet the director. He excused himself, and though Nancy knew she was just a freshman reporter and he was a staff member, she couldn't help feeling competitive with Jake. She didn't have time to process this, however, because just then Brian pulled her aside.

"Nancy," he said urgently. "I've got to talk

with you. After I get changed, I'm going out for a quick dinner with my parents before they head back home, but I'll be at the Kappa party later." He glanced around as if he was afraid that someone might be listening. "I need your help with something important, something very private. I've got to go now, but can you get Bess to fill you in on the details?"

Just as Nancy opened her mouth to speak, Brian disappeared with his parents.

What is going on here? Nancy asked herself, not for the first time that evening.

"Talk about Party Central," Eileen said, trying to sound cheerful as they headed up the Kappa house front walk.

"Oh, yes. This is what we came for," Ginny said, her eyes lighting up. Already there were partygoers spilling out on Kappa's front porch, and the lawn was jammed.

"When the action starts before the front door, that's a good sign," Reva added happily, holding Andy Rodriguez's hand as they stepped over a cluster of students sitting on the porch steps.

If only I had a date, Eileen thought enviously as she followed her friends through Kappa's front door and watched several couples sweep by. There was Liz, talking to Daniel. And Kara was sitting on Tim Downing's lap, feeding him potato chips. As Eileen took note of the paired-up partygoers, her eardrums throbbed. The full force of the music from Ray's band, the Beat Poets, was blasting from the backyard through the house. She could see bodies jammed everywhere, and a smile spread across her face. Well, even if she didn't have a date, there was no doubt that the Kappa party was the place to be. And there were definitely enough good-looking guys swarming around here. Who knew? Maybe she'd meet some handsome guy who'd fall madly in love with her.

Feeling cheerier, she started looking around for her friends and moved into the crowd. Dodging as some football players barreled through the jam-packed room, she made her way to the soda fountain area.

"You pledges have something to be proud of," said one of the upper-class sisters as she pressed behind her on her way to the keg. "I've never seen decorations this cool."

Eileen beamed. Oh, she was going to have a good time tonight.

"Oh, Eileen, there you are," Casey said, flashing her a bright grin. She was dancing with two cute guys from the cast.

Some people have luck oozing out of every pore, Eileen thought enviously as she managed a weak smile for Casey.

"Oops, sorry," Eileen muttered as she bumped into someone. The next second she almost went into shock as she realized that she'd just bumped into Paul Cody, the drop-dead gorgeous guy she'd met at Melina Stavros's discussion group.

"Hey, it's you," he said, giving her the full benefit of a row of even white teeth.

Maybe it's my turn for some luck, Eileen thought. "Hey, Paul," she said, hoping she sounded casual.

"Don't tell me. You're the girl from Political Theory, right?" he asked. "Eileen, that's it, right?"

Pleased at being remembered, Eileen preened a little. She tried to smile in what she hoped was a flirtatious way.

"You might show up late for discussions, but I see you're right on time for the party, and you have your names straight," she said.

Paul smiled appreciatively. "I have my priorities in the right place. And the next priority on my list is a dance with you. What do you say?"

She was about to say yes when she felt a hand on her arm.

"There you are." It was Soozie Beckerman. "I've been rounding up the pledges. We are absolutely running out of everything. Can you believe it? Get to the kitchen and refill the refreshment bowls—pronto. And someone already spilled sticky soda on one of our sofas. Can you see that it gets cleaned up?"

Eileen gulped and looked from Soozie to Paul. "I—uh," she stammered.

Soozie raised an eyebrow, but then her look

softened as her gaze fell on Paul. She studied his well-built frame appreciatively. "Eileen's busy, but I'm not. Come with me," she said firmly, taking Paul's arm and leading him through the living room.

Paul turned around and gave Eileen a helpless look before being swallowed up by the crowd.

Being a pledge is the pits, Eileen thought with a sigh as she made her way toward the kitchen. It wasn't that she minded helping, but did Soozie's timing have to be so bad? She'd probably lost any chance of hooking up with Paul. And people like Casey managed to have two guys interested in them at the same time. It wasn't fair!

The word *fair* came once again to Eileen's mind as she made her way into the snack area with a tray of food. She spotted Casey talking in the corner of the room with several cast members. Soozie was standing nearby, wearing Paul on her arm like an ornament. It was clear to Eileen that Soozie hadn't insisted that Casey help serve refreshments. She bet no one had asked her to clean up sticky soda spills, either!

"Hey, Casey, can you lend a hand?" Eileen asked. She set the tray down on a low table next to the laughing girl.

"Sure, in a minute," Casey said, reaching for a handful of pretzels and not missing a beat in the story she was telling about Charley Stern, her TV star boyfriend. Her audience chuckled appreciatively.

"In a minute," Eileen mimicked, feeling miffed as she headed back to the kitchen to reload.

"This is unbelievable," George gasped, staring at Nancy and Bess as she sat on the tiled bathroom counter in the powder room at the back of the sorority house. "Brian's gay? And being black-mailed?"

"Lower your voice," Bess warned, leaning up against the bathroom door. It had been her idea to gather her friends in the only place in the crowded Kappa house where they could talk.

"Don't worry, there's no danger of anyone hearing a thing with that music amped up the way it is," Nancy replied.

"So say something, George," Bess urged.

"Give me a second to get used to this, okay? This is a lot of news to absorb. All right, so Brian and Chris are a couple, which is cool. But black-mailing's not cool. So any ideas about who's the blackmailer?" George said, darting looks at Bess and Nancy.

"Your guess is as good as mine," Bess said. "But we've got to figure it out. You saw Brian tonight. He's becoming a total wreck."

"Who else knows he's gay?" Nancy asked.

"No one," Bess answered promptly.

George frowned at her cousin. "Someone must," she pointed out. "Has anyone even hinted out loud about his homosexuality?"

"Well," Bess said slowly, "now that you mention

it, during rush, some of the sorority sisters gave me the business about not dating Brian. I don't really remember what they said, but Soozie, well, she was kind of throwing these little zingers out about him, like she was getting at something. I didn't make much of it at the time, but now, I don't know. Maybe there's something there."

"So suppose it's Soozie," Nancy said. "Why would she want to blackmail Brian?"

Bess shook her head. "She seems to have plenty of money. Every time I see her, she's wearing something expensive, and she drives a brand-new BMW."

"So, okay, maybe she doesn't need the money," George suggested. "But she might want to get back at Brian for some reason. Maybe she's jealous of him."

"I'd believe that of some other people," Bess said. "I mean after all, Brian was one of the few freshmen to be chosen for a part. And some of the students who didn't make it were pretty upset. But Soozie wouldn't care about that, and anyway I don't think she even knows him personally."

"Who else was at that rush party?" asked George. "Was Eileen? I saw her glaring at Brian while she was serving refreshments just before you dragged me in here for this conference."

"Well, maybe," Bess mumbled. She didn't like the idea that a fellow pledge would mastermind a blackmail plot. "She can be moody sometimes, but she doesn't seem to have any reason, either."

"Well, we have to consider everyone, even if it doesn't seem to make sense," Nancy said thoughtfully. "Who else, Bess?"

George watched Bess staring into the bathroom mirror, trying to come up with a thought. Bess turned and said, "There's one other guy. A freshman named Erik Grenquist. I don't really know him, but he blew up at Brian last night during rehearsal—and all Brian did was bump him when he walked by. And then right before the play, I saw him snap a picture of Brian."

"Why would he be taking pictures?" Nancy jumped on that bit of information.

Bess shrugged. "I don't know. I never saw him with a camera before. He always hung around rehearsals even though he wasn't in the show. Then someone let him work on props. He was so pathetically grateful that I felt sorry for him until I saw how angry he got when Brian bumped him."

"Find out more about him," George said decisively. "Maybe he's got some hidden reason for wanting to hurt Brian."

"Poor Brian," Bess said softly. "He looks awful tonight. I saw him standing by the champagne table just kind of staring off into space. Here's our opening celebration, and he looks like he wishes the ground would swallow him up."

"Well, the celebration is still going on, and we're sitting here in the bathroom," George said suddenly. "I'd better get back or Will is going to think I abandoned him."

"Jake will think the same thing about me," Nancy said, jumping up.

"And I'm supposed to be hosting this event," Bess said, and she threw open the door.

"My, are things that crowded that three of you have to jam into one little bathroom?" Soozie said, her face unreadable, after the three of them had emerged.

Nancy scanned Soozie's face but couldn't tell if Soozie had heard anything. And in an instant Soozie stepped into the bathroom and closed the door behind her.

"Isn't she a peach?" Bess said sarcastically.

George gave Nancy a worried look, but just then three cast members spotted Bess.

"A-ha!" they shouted triumphantly, and pulled her toward the dance floor. "We've been looking for you all night. Where have you been hiding?"

"There you are," Will called. His eyes met George's, and she smiled lovingly.

"Sorry," she said. "I was waylaid by some friends."

"Well, I guess we need to make up for some lost time. How about we find a corner of the dance floor and claim it as ours?"

Nancy watched George and Will disappear, then made her way through the crush, searching for Jake. She finally spotted him studying the titles through the window of the rainbow jukebox the pledges had rented.

"Hi," she said, coming up behind him.

A song Nancy recognized from an oldies station belted out from the speakers then. She guessed that the Beat Poets were taking a break and that the music from the jukebox was filling in.

"Want to dance?" Jake asked. He pulled Nancy out onto the dance floor. He was such a natural dancer that she quickly found herself moving in perfect time with him. Before long she forgot all about Brian and his troubles. Her senses were totally filled with the nearness of Jake and the pulsing beat of the music. By now the party was really heating up. The room was becoming so crowded, it was hard to maneuver. Every inch was filled with bodies. Through the crush, Nancy spotted Brian, and he appeared upset.

"I can't figure it out," Jake said into her ear. "A million compliments about his performance and Brian still looks like forty miles of bad road. What's going on with him? It can't be stage fright. The show's over—for tonight anyway."

Nancy glanced up at Jake, wanting to explain, but she'd promised not to tell anyone. The magic of dancing with Jake faded away as she found herself focusing again on Brian's problem.

"Jake, do you mind? There's someone I have to talk to."

"Now?" Nancy winced at the hurt that flashed across Jake's eyes.

"It's really important," Nancy said.

Jake waved a hand. "No problem. I actually think I'm getting used to this."

"Sorry. I'll be right back," Nancy promised.

She left the dance floor. "Brian!" she called.

Brian's head jerked up as he heard his name. But just as Nancy was about to reach him, he was pulled onto the dance floor by one of the girls she recognized from the cast.

Figures, Nancy muttered. She stopped and watched Brian, who seemed to be drowning in the sea of writhing bodies. Just as she was about to turn away, she heard someone say, "I hate that guy, Brian. Guys like him have no business being at Wilder."

Nancy's head whipped around as she tried to sort out who had just spoken, but there were too many people crowded around. The voice could have belonged to any one of them.

CHAPTER 6

Nancy studied the crowd, feeling a surge of frustration. But then she heard the voice again, and she zeroed in on its owner, a guy standing by the wall. He was a pale, slender young man with heavy brows and a thick thatch of light brown hair.

Now, what did he mean, "guys like Brian," Nancy wondered, studying the man intently.

"Bess," she whispered urgently, grabbing her cousin's arm as she passed. "Do you know who that guy in the brown sweater is?"

"Erik. Erik Grenquist," Bess said. "The one I told you about who got so angry at Brian during rehearsal. The one who helped with the props for the play."

"Let's go talk with him," Nancy whispered.

"Don't waste your time—he's got as much personality as a—" Bess started to say, but Nancy grabbed her and led her toward Erik.

"This is about *Brian*," Nancy hissed.

"Hi," Nancy said brightly to Erik. "I heard you were in charge of the props, and I just wanted to say that I thought they were spectacular. Really helped make the show."

"What?" Erik asked, sounding stunned.

"No, I mean it," Nancy said, talking a mile a minute. She was aware that Bess was staring at her, but she pressed on. "You see, I go to the theater a lot, and most people don't realize that having the right props can really make or break a production. You seem to know what you're doing. Not too many people have the touch."

Erik responded almost pathetically to the flattery. He drew himself up and nodded. "Yeah. You're right. Some people think you have to act in the play to count." He looked over at Bess. "But I happen to know it's what's going on behind the scenes that counts. Not that I don't want to be onstage."

"You're a freshman, right?" Bess asked, taking Nancy's cue and groping for something—anything—to say.

"Yes," Erik muttered. "And you don't have to rub it in. I already know there was only one freshman guy who got a part—Brian Daglian."

He almost spat out the name, and Nancy felt her heart beating faster. She darted a glance at Bess.

"You were in the chorus, weren't you?" Erik asked, his eyes zeroing in on Bess.

Bess nodded.

"Another freshman, and you got a part." It was almost an accusation.

"Well," Bess said lamely, "I guess I got lucky."

"Whatever," Erik muttered. "Next year at this time, I won't be stuck behind the scenes—nor in any anonymous spot in the chorus." With that, he strode off.

Nancy turned to Bess. "I guess he told you," she said with a laugh.

Bess shook her head. "I told you he was a strange guy. So, did our visit with him tell you anything?"

Nancy became thoughtful. "It was hard to get a read on him to see if he was our blackmailer, from the little he said."

"True," Bess replied. "I'm still kind of wondering myself. Here comes Brian. Let's ask him if thinks there's a chance Erik's the one."

Brian scowled when Nancy pointed out Erik and asked him if it were possible that he was the blackmailer.

"That wuss?" Brian smirked. "He made it clear that he was jealous that I got a part and he didn't, but I don't know. I doubt he'd go all out to try to wreck my life because of it."

"Brian, are you still upset because your folks came to see the performance?" Bess asked with concern.

"Not exactly." Brian lowered his voice and glanced around the crowded room. "I found some more photos and another note in my bag in the dressing room."

"Let's go outside and talk about this," Nancy said.

She led them out back and away from a group of people. Brian pulled a small blue plastic envelope out of his jacket pocket. He handed it to Nancy.

Nancy opened the envelope, pulling out two photos showing Chris giving Brian a small box. Then she unfolded the note. It was a computer print-out that said, "Smile! You boys are on film for all the world to see—if I want it to & if you don't mail $500 to the usual P.O. box."

Nancy turned the note over to see if there was anything written on the back.

"This blackmailing creep is really getting on my nerves," she said grimly.

Brian pushed his hair back in an agitated manner. "You and me both," he said. "My parents were outside the dressing room, waiting for me when I found this. I almost got sick. Luckily, my mom thought I was pale from nerves, so I played that one up."

"Your acting talents paid off," Bess said dryly.

"Yeah," Brian muttered. "And now I've got to pay up. I've sent more money to good old P.O. box 2090 than you can believe."

"This note doesn't tell us much," Nancy said,

still examining it. "But the fact that the post office box is in town is one clue. When did you mail the last payment?"

Brian scowled. "I just sent the payment money for the videotape yesterday," he said darkly.

Nancy thought a minute, then seemed to make up her mind about something. "Well, the money should be at the P.O. box in Weston by tomorrow," she said. "Tell you what. I've got to head into Weston to run some errands anyway, so maybe I can keep an eye on the post office box to see if anyone picks up the money. If I remember right, there's a huge plate-glass window in the front of the post office. Maybe I'll catch whoever's doing this in the act."

It seemed to Eileen that she'd be stuck forever doing refreshment duty. Once or twice she spotted Paul Cody across the crowded room. He was never lacking for female company. And no wonder, Eileen thought with a scowl. He was probably the best-looking guy around. She studied his strong profile and his well-muscled body. Then she sighed. If only she could get away long enough to talk to him. At last she got her chance. She darted over to the counter where Paul was filling up a cup from the soda fountain.

"Hey, go easy on the fizzy stuff," she said lightly.

Paul turned around, giving her the full effect

of his eyes. "There you are. I've been looking for you."

Eileen smiled, but before she could open her mouth to speak, the music stopped and Soozie leaped up and gestured for attention. She was holding a microphone, and her voice boomed around the room. "Pledges—it's skit time."

"That's me." Eileen tried not to wail with disappointment. Reluctantly, she left Paul and ran to join the other pledges in the dining room, where they assembled.

"Places, everyone," Casey said.

I can't believe I'm doing this, Eileen thought to herself. It wasn't that she didn't love Kappa, but the thought of going onstage made her stomach start doing weird jumping jacks. How could Bess and the rest of the *Grease!* cast have ever gotten up on stage in front of that huge audience? Quickly, the pledges hurried to the makeshift stage set up in the backyard near the band. As she was headed out to the stage, Eileen saw Paul, her heart thumping wildly. Oh, please don't let me look too stupid in front of him.

"Welcome, everyone, to the Kappa pledges' version of *Grease!,* starring our 'upperclasswomen,' " Bess announced.

The guys in Ray's band started playing a distorted version of *Grease!* as one of the pledges leaped out onto the stage wearing a wig the exact shade of Holly's hair. Another pledge stepped out wearing a distinctive outfit everyone recognized as belonging to the sorority's vice-president. The crowd clapped and laughed.

"Oh, look, there's Soozie," someone shouted as Casey strutted out on stage. The audience howled appreciatively. It seemed that no one could mistake her sauntering walk. Eileen saw that Soozie was laughing and felt relieved. Almost everyone in the Kappa house had a good sense of humor, but Eileen had been sure that Soozie would be upset about being parodied. Of course, she reasoned, if it had been anyone but the star of *The President's Daughter* ...

When it was Eileen's turn, she walked woodenly on stage, knowing every eye was on her.

Eileen felt her cheeks burn when she caught her toe in a crack on the stage and nearly fell. Great. She'd just made it out on stage and already messed up. Someone cranked out a sped-up version of the *Grease!* soundtrack and the pledges lip-synched, doing exaggerated dance steps and crashing into one another. Through it all, Eileen felt that her body had a will of its own and wouldn't do anything right. The other girls, she felt, carried the parody off perfectly. The audience was laughing and calling out to the actresses, the Kappa sisters loudest of all. Casey and Bess were natural performers and were really hamming it up. Here I am, completely mortified, and they're actually enjoying themselves, Eileen thought incredulously.

Finally, just when Eileen thought she might

burst into tears, the performance mercifully ended. She started off the stage, oblivious to the laughter and shouts of "Way to go!" Her eyes were on Paul, who was standing just to the left of the stage. At last she had her chance. To heck with Soozie and serving refreshments. She was going to enjoy herself.

Eileen was just about to walk over to Paul when she noticed that his eyes had moved past her. She turned around to see who he was look-ing at and saw that it was Bess. "What a hoot!" Bess exclaimed.

Eileen watched in distress as she saw Paul make his way over to Bess. She bolted for the back door of the sorority house. Who was she kidding? She didn't belong here. Kappa was for winners, and as far as she was concerned, she was a complete loser with a capital *L*.

"You were fabulous!" Bess said, hugging Casey.

"I was laughing so hard, I had tears in my eyes and could barely see where I was going. Was that your foot I stepped on?" Casey asked.

"Yes, but I got over it." Bess smiled. "Just don't let it happen again."

Casey grew serious. "Do you think the sisters liked it?"

Bess lowered her voice. "We knocked 'em dead."

"Hi," said a deep male voice from behind Bess.

She looked over her shoulder and took in a full dose of his bronzed body and sandy brown hair.

"Hi, yourself," she said politely. After all, she was one of the hostesses of this event. "Did you enjoy the show?"

Bess watched as the handsome guy smiled at Casey. Oh, dear, she thought. Another one of Casey's starstruck, adoring fans. She stood back to let Casey do the talking.

"My name is Paul Cody," the guy continued, ignoring Casey as he spoke to Bess. "And you're Bess Marvin. I saw your name in the program."

He's talking to *me,* Bess realized. Casey grinned and shot Bess a knowing wink, then excused herself. Bess was left to make conversation with Paul. Not a bad assignment, she thought. As they talked, she realized that he was nice as well as cute.

"You guys did a great job with the play," Paul said. "I saw a stage production in Chicago a few months ago that all the critics raved about. It's a great musical. A lot of fun."

"It must have been cool to see that show. I read all about it," Bess said enviously.

"It was. Especially for me. I'm a complete theater hound," Paul said, nodding.

Ordinarily, Bess would have thought she'd died and gone to heaven, but now, standing out in the Kappa yard talking with one of the cutest guys around, she was surprised to find herself remembering her vow to buckle down and get her

grades up. She had no time for guys—even total
babes like Paul. She had to keep up her grades
if she was going to be allowed to participate in
any more Wilder drama productions. And pledging was no small-time commitment, either. Also,
now she had to help Brian out of the blackmail
mess he was in.

"So listen, I hate to rush off," she said reluctantly—after all, there was no denying Paul was
cute—"but I've got some stuff to do. It was nice
talking with you."

Nancy was filling up her cup at the soda fountain when she heard Soozie next to her.

"Did you see how Eileen nearly tripped?" she
hooted to her friends.

"Was she the one who looked like she was
ready to die up there?" someone asked.

"Yes," Soozie answered. "I don't think dear
Eileen is cut out to be a performer."

Nancy turned and sipped while she studied
Soozie. She had to find out more about her. But
there was probably no point in trying to talk to
her now. Soozie definitely led any conversation.
Still, there were other ways.

Nancy went up the stairs. She turned as if she
were heading for the bathroom but was really
checking to see that the coast was clear. She
walked down the hallway and peered into several
rooms until she found the one she was looking
for—with a bed on which there was a pillow em-

broidered with the name *Soozie*. She slipped inside the room and gazed around.

At first glance she saw nothing of interest. The bed had a flowered bedspread and more throw pillows, some embroidered with the Kappa crest. A small desk had a sleek laptop computer and lots of photos of blond Soozie and her sorority sisters at various parties. Nancy peered intently at the photos, but they told her nothing. Moving on, Nancy inspected the closet, since the doors were open. She could see that the closet was jammed with expensive clothes. The bookshelves were filled with the usual textbooks. But then something caught Nancy's eye—a high school yearbook.

"Now, maybe this could be revealing," Nancy murmured. Pulling it out, she realized that it was from Brian's hometown. Hmm, she thought, flipping through it, maybe Soozie and Brian knew each other after all.

Just then she heard the door creak open behind her and she jumped.

"Nancy, what are you doing?"

Relieved, Nancy saw that it was Jake. Guiltily, she slipped the yearbook back in the shelf.

"Oh, nothing," she said, not meeting his eyes.

"Nothing?" Jake said in a puzzled voice. "This is kind of an odd place to go to do nothing."

"It—it was just getting to be so loud downstairs." Nancy tried to sound convincing. "I don't know—I just ended up here."

She felt her heart pound as she gazed into Jake's eyes and became aware that they were burning with intensity. The yearbook and her mission were quickly forgotten. The moonlight was spilling in the window, and Nancy was mesmerized by how it lit up Jake's features and played resplendently across his face. He was so incredibly handsome—even with his hair messed up from dancing. Actually, Nancy realized, she liked it that way.

Jake moved toward her, his eyes never leaving her face. "Nancy," he said in a husky voice. "Look at me." Then he reached and pulled her closer to him, and Nancy took in the warmth of his body and the faint lemony smell of his aftershave. Her senses began to reel as he tilted her chin.

"Nancy, I—" he began.

The next minute the romantic mood was shattered as several shouts of "It's not fair! It's not fair" tore through the night air. These were followed by rising voices calling, "Who are those people?" and "What do those signs say?"

Nancy broke away from Jake's hold and stepped back abruptly. "What is that?"

Jake shrugged and tried to pick up where they'd left off. Part of Nancy wanted to melt back into his arms, but as the shouting continued, her curiosity overcame her. She pulled back again and listened to the loud chanting.

Finally Jake strode over to the window, the

steel tips of his cowboy boots glinting in the moonlight.

"Check this out," he murmured.

Nancy raced to the window and looked down to see a number of students who hadn't been at the Kappa party earlier, all brandishing picket signs with sayings on them like, Equality for All!, Unfair to Wilder Students!, Down with Elitism!

Her eyes grew wide. "I don't believe this," she gasped. "Where did these people come from? Why are they trying to ruin the opening night party with some sort of protest?"

"*Trying* is not the word," Jake said. "They seem to be succeeding."

CHAPTER 7

Jake stood next to Nancy and watched from the window as more pickets appeared and the chanting intensified. They seemed to be coming from all directions.

"Who are those people?" Jake asked.

Nancy shook her head. "There sure are a lot of them."

A number of pickets began gathering on the driveway, while several pickets marched over by the stage where the Beat Poets were set up.

Jake saw Ray motion to his band members to cut the music. The partygoers stopped dancing and stared at the pickets, who were walking in circles and brandishing their signs.

"Get out of here," Jake heard someone yell above the din. He could see Bess and some of the pledges huddled by the stage, plainly confused and upset.

"Jake, this is unbelievable," Nancy said.

"You're telling me," Jake muttered, pulling her closer. He didn't want this moment interrupted, pickets or no pickets.

"I've got to go down there," Nancy said abruptly.

"No, don't." Jake couldn't believe what he was hearing. "What does this have to do with you? This isn't your sorority. This isn't your problem."

"Jake, please try to understand. I want to go to see if there's anything I can do. My friends are there," Nancy said as she looked into Jake's eyes.

So what am I supposed to say? Jake thought, dropping his arms to his sides. That I wish you'd leave them to their protesting, and let me kiss you as I've been dying to all night? But Nancy had turned and was gone.

"Fine, no problem," Jake muttered to the empty room. He looked around. Only seconds before the moonlight had spilled inside, creating a romantic atmosphere just for them, the room electric with possibility. Now as Jake paced back and forth by the window, the light seemed cold and loveless. He looked down on the activity below and spotted Nancy pushing through to Bess and her friends.

"Well, Collins, what exactly was that all about?" Jake sat heavily on Soozie's bed without giving any thought to the fact that he was trespassing in a stranger's bedroom. "I mean, one minute Nancy's here, giving off the signals you've been hoping for—the next, she's out there."

Moodily, he studied the rectangle of moonlight sliding across the floor. It hadn't escaped his notice that Nancy had been slipping away from him the entire evening. It seemed that all he'd done during the party was search for her. What was going on? The empty room gave him no answers and even seemed to mock his questions. He closed his eyes and mentally completed the tableau of his kissing Nancy, placing his hand against the back of that graceful, sloping neck and—it was no use. None of this made sense.

"Maybe getting involved with her wasn't such a good idea," Jake chided himself. He should have paid attention to the little voice telling him not to get too close to Nancy, to leave things as they were—strictly business. Sighing heavily, he stood up and walked out. There was no doubt that she was keeping something from him. Well, he wouldn't press it—for now.

"Do you believe this?" Bess exclaimed to Nancy as they stood together on the driveway looking at the pandemonium caused by the pickets. Several of the partygoers who'd obviously had too much beer started jeering at the pickets.

"Get a life!" someone shouted.

One of the guys sent a full can of beer spiraling into the crowd, drenching several students holding picket signs. Someone hurled a toilet paper roll from an upstairs bathroom. It unfurled and landed on a couple of protesters. Two other guys grabbed a sign and started running through the crowd shouting, "Talk about unfair. They didn't bring enough picket signs for us all!"

"Ignore the Greek slob," yelled one of the pickets. "What can you expect?"

The chanting picked up in intensity. Bess started counting. There were at least twenty-five women waving signs. The Beat Poets had started packing up their instruments so they wouldn't get damaged. The whole party had come to a screeching halt.

Bess studied her friends anxiously. The party was being ruined. And to make things even worse, this was the first opening night of the Wilder Drama Department theater season. What a great opening night party! Talk about unfair! All the hard work she and her fellow pledges had put in was for nothing. She felt her frustration rise. If only these pickets would just leave. Sighing, she turned as Casey appeared at her elbow.

"What a disaster," Casey muttered.

"You're telling me," Bess said.

"I'm the cause of all this," Casey said unhappily.

Then one of the picket-carrying students spotted her. "So, Casey Fontaine, is this what they call star treatment?" she taunted.

Casey's hands flew up to her reddened cheeks. "It's not what you think," she retorted hotly.

The picket shot her a look. "Things are never what they seem," she said, but then she laughed.

What was so funny? Bess wondered, then swooped in to protect her friend. "Leave her alone!" Bess shouted.

Casey darted a wild look at Bess, then bolted for the protection of the Kappa house. She side-stepped Holly as the president stepped out on the back porch.

"Why don't you crawl back under the rocks you came from!" Bess yelled at the pickets.

"Shhh," Holly said, placing a hand on Bess's shoulder. "Don't sink to their level." She turned toward the advancing group.

"Listen up! We're taking this up with the Pan-hellenic Council," she called. She received several catcalls in return, and she held up a hand to silence the crowd. Bess was amazed that the noise level actually died down.

"This is really nobody's business but our own. This only involves our sorority. Could you all just go and leave us alone?"

The catcalls grew louder, and Bess could see that no one had any intention of leaving.

"Tell us something we don't already know," one girl shouted at Holly.

"They must have found out about the formal complaint," someone whispered to Bess.

"But how?" Bess asked. Puzzled, she more closely studied the crowd of pickets who had resumed their shouts and taunts. "They're all girls," she said, more to herself than to anybody else. What was more, she noticed, some of them seemed to be trying very hard not to laugh. Something was definitely fishy about this protest!

The next morning Brian sat on his bed in his dorm room, staring gloomily at the phone. Once or twice he reached for the receiver, only to put it back. They're going to think I've got an out-of-control spending thing going, he thought. His parents gave him a generous allowance, but there was no way that it could cover the demands the blackmailer was making.

Brian rehearsed what he was going to say, "Hi, Dad, it's me, Brian." He'd ask his dad about the election, then lay out his request. No, he'd just plunge right in and get it over with. "I hope you don't mind, but I really need more money for some school projects I'm working on," he continued, rehearsing while trying to work up the courage to call. Finally, he gave a huge sigh and punched in the numbers.

As he waited for someone to pick up, Brian closed his eyes and imagined his house. His mom would be just getting back from her low-impact aerobics class, while his dad would be settling down to work at his computer. That's it—the computer, Brian thought as his dad answered the phone. That will be my excuse.

"Brian!" his dad said eagerly, which caused Brian a stab of guilt. His dad wouldn't be so glad to hear from him when he found out that he was going to ask for more cash. Sure enough, his father's voice lost its eagerness when Brian explained the purpose of the call. "Well, sure, Brian. But what happened to the money we gave you?"

"Well, it's my computer hard drive," Brian said hurriedly. "It—it got totally fried. We had this weird power surge in the dorms. Old wiring and all, you know. Anyway, I forgot to mention it last night, but I lost all my files and everything. The technician said there was no fixing it."

Brian hoped he'd sounded believable. "Well, okay, Bri," his father said, but Brian detected a note of uncertainty.

He knows I'm lying. He can always see right through me.

"Everything else going okay?"

"Fine, fine," Brian lied. "Anything new going on with the election?"

"Well, I just got off the phone with my campaign manager," Mr. Daglian said. "He says we've got our work cut out for us. This election's much closer than we'd imagined. My opponent put out some story about my finances that we can easily prove untrue. Still, it's caused some problem, as you might well guess."

"Oh," Brian said weakly.

"But as long as there are no other surprises, I think I'm positioned pretty well."

If only you knew what surprise just might happen, Brian thought.

After he hung up the phone, he put his head in his hands and sat that way for a long time.

Nancy woke up after a dream-filled, fitful sleep. She lay in bed for a few minutes, while Kara slumbered on peacefully, and thought about the strange events of the night before. First, she allowed her mind to wander over the picketing that had gone on at the Kappa party. Who were those people, and why had they chosen that particular time to stage a protest? Well, actually, it was obvious. The pickets wanted to be sure they had an audience when they decided to get their point across.

After a while Nancy's thoughts drifted to Jake. She tried to remember how it had felt to be held in his strong arms. She wondered vaguely what it would have felt like to be kissed by him. But that look he'd given her just before she'd taken off to help out her friends wasn't good. She didn't want to think about Jake right then.

She continued on to Brian's dilemma. In her mind she turned over the few clues she had, but came up with nothing. She had to know more if she were to have a chance at helping him and Bess figure out who the blackmailer was. That video she'd heard about might yield more information.

Nancy sprang out of bed. She'd better get going if she was going to be of any help to poor Brian. Immediately after she showered, she called him. The phone rang and rang. Finally he answered.

"What?" His voice was curt.

"Hi, it's Nancy. Sorry to call so early after such a big night, but I've been thinking over your situation. There must be something here that we're all missing. I really think I ought to take a look at that video."

"Well, okay . . ." Brian wavered. It was clear he was still uncomfortable about anyone seeing it.

"Brian, I know this is all pretty sensitive," Nancy said in gentle voice. "I wouldn't ask you this if I didn't think it might really help us figure out this mess."

"I just talked with my dad this morning," Brian burst out. "He keeps saying how his election is so close. This whole thing is doing a real number on my mind."

"We're going to put a stop to it," Nancy said firmly. "But I need your help. You'll have to let me look at the video."

"All right," Brian agreed after a lengthy pause. They made plans to meet on campus at noon and hung up.

Hearing noises out in the lounge, Nancy walked out to see if there was any more news about the protest. She saw Reva and Ginny draped across the sofa. Dawn was seated in the deep chair by the TV and Casey was sitting cross-legged on the floor, obviously still very upset.

"Too bad I missed the action," Reva said as she applied deep purple polish to her toenails. "I went to Andy's just after the skit."

"You didn't miss much," Ginny replied. "Just your basic mob scene."

"I caused a lot of trouble," Casey said softly.

"No, you didn't," Reva stated emphatically. "If I recall, Kappa came after you—you didn't go bashing down their door."

"I never intended to cause so many problems," Casey said.

"I don't know," Dawn said. "I mean, you kind of knew they were bending the rules for you, and you didn't stop them."

Casey looked wounded, but she appeared to consider Dawn's words. "So what do I do?"

Dawn shrugged. "I'm not the right person to ask. I think the whole Greek thing is weird in the first place."

"No offense," Kara said, "I like you," Casey, but there's no getting around the fact that there were students who rushed but didn't get chosen by a sorority."

Nancy wanted to step to Casey's defense, but realized she didn't have much to say. It wasn't exactly fair, and yet she really cared for Casey and didn't want her to be hurt.

Eileen came into the lounge then. Good, thought Nancy. Eileen will step in and say something. But when Eileen's eyes took in Casey, she turned and left the suite without a word.

Go figure, Nancy thought in disbelief. Casey's own pledge sister! You'd think Eileen would have said something to make her feel better.

"Did you ever see such a pigsty?" Bess asked as she stooped to pick up yet another can.

"I'm glad we're almost finished," one of the other pledges complained. "This was the mother of all messes. I'm sticky and gross and will probably need two showers to come clean."

"Those pickets didn't help matters," Bess muttered, watching one of the pledges mop up the dried beer on the porch, then sitting down on the back steps.

"Talk about a nightmare," another pledge added.

Bess looked over at Casey, who had spent the last hour or so silently helping clean up after the party. Bess knew Casey was feeling terrible. Casey had told her that earlier that morning some of the women in Casey's suite had talked with her about the protest, and some of them had mentioned that the rules had been bent for her.

It seemed like days since *Grease!* and the excitement of opening night. Now the whole Kappa house was steeped in gloom over the "Casey thing," as she'd heard several of the sisters refer to it. A couple of the Kappa sisters, including Soozie and Holly, came out and sat on the rails.

"We'd better figure what to do about our situation," Soozie said.

"We could just wait for the Panhellenic Council meeting and lay everything out," one of the sisters ventured.

"Some of the council members belong to other sororities who are jealous of us," another pointed out. "We might not get a very fair hearing."

"I thought I recognized a couple of those pickets. I think they were from some other sorority," added someone else.

Holly furrowed her brow. "The strange thing about the Panhellenic review is that normally the council requests that the officers from the sorority come to speak. This time, they requested that we send a pledge."

Soozie glowered. "That's ridiculous. A pledge couldn't possibly handle an important matter like this."

Holly replied, "Well, that's who they asked for. I think Bess would be a good choice."

Bess became horror-stricken. "Me!"

"Yes, you're closest to Casey, and I think you'd state our case very well," Holly replied.

"A *pledge* stating our case! This whole situation has gotten out of hand," Soozie retorted. "I simply won't stand for it. And the first chance I get, I'll tell Panhellenic."

Casey stood up. "There will be no situation because there's only one solution. I'm dropping out."

With that, she walked around the driveway to the front and let herself out the side gate.

CHAPTER 8

Bess sat stunned as Casey disappeared after delivering her bomb.

"Stop her," Soozie commanded Bess.

"I think she wants to be alone—" another Kappa said, but was cut off by the look in Soozie's eyes.

Bess leaped up and took off down the driveway, running to overtake Casey on the sidewalk in front of the Pi Phi house. Out of the corner of her eye she saw Kara standing on Pi Phi's porch with a group of other women, and she waved distractedly as she continued pursuing Casey. Bess noted that Kara and the others seemed more than a little interested in what was going on with her and Casey. Still, Bess didn't have time to wonder what that was all about. She had to stop Casey.

"Casey, wait," she called.

Casey slowed but didn't turn around. Bess fell in next to her, puffing while she tried to talk. "Casey, at least—wait until Panhellenic—makes a decision. You—can't just—quit."

Casey jerked her chin up. "I just did."

"C'mon—come back. Let's—all talk this over."

"I've already said what needed to be said."

"Casey, think about it—please?"

"I've given it plenty of thought."

"But, Casey," Bess pleaded, "we've all been through a lot together. You can't just quit because things are a little rough right now."

"A *little* rough?" Casey shot back, and doubled her speed. Bess clutched at her aching side while she puffed and tried to keep up with Casey's pace. Jeez, she was out of shape. It might be a good idea to join George in her morning runs.

"Bess, you're wasting your time. Go back to the Kappa house and tell them nothing's changing my mind. I don't want to cause any more problems."

Deflated, Bess stopped and watched as Casey disappeared. I never realized how stubborn Casey can be, Bess thought as she turned and walked back to the Kappa house. Well, never mind. We'll get her to change her mind somehow.

"Where is she?" Soozie demanded of Bess when she returned. "You were supposed to bring her back."

Bess let out a sigh. "She wouldn't listen to me. She said she quit and that was that."

"She'd better not quit," Soozie said, giving Bess a measured stare.

"Maybe she'll cool off and see things differently," Bess said.

Soozie seemed about to say something else when several other upperclasswomen walked into the room, followed by a couple of pledges.

"This whole thing is stupid, if you ask me," one woman muttered. She examined her fingernails as she added, "I guess we did bend the rules. It just made everything simpler that Casey quit."

"That's not right," said another Kappa emphatically. "Since when do we let jerks like those pickets tell us what to?"

A couple of girls agreed.

"We need Casey in this sorority," Soozie said grimly. "Every sorority house would die to have a TV star as a member."

Bess ignored that and added, "Maybe it wasn't quite fair. But Casey is such a great person that she's an asset to any sorority, even if she weren't a TV star."

Soozie glared at her. "You just don't get it, do you?" With that she flounced out.

"What was that all about?" Bess asked. "I thought we were on the same side. Soozie wants Casey in the sorority, doesn't she?"

"Yes," said Holly. "I just think her reasons for

wanting Casey to stay with Kappa are a bit different from yours."

"Can you spell *prestige?*" another sister said.

"Well, there's no doubt having a TV star is kind of a feather in our caps."

"My friend Sheila wanted to rush, but she was told she'd missed the deadline and would have to wait until next fall," said Kim, one of the pledges.

Bess darted a look at her. Kim had a point. If only this issue weren't so complicated.

"Well, the whole thing is completely out of hand," one pledge said. "And I'm sick to death of it. It's just another way for Casey Fontaine to draw attention to herself. I guess being on TV and having a hot star like Charley Stern for a boyfriend wasn't enough for her. Now she's got to cause trouble for Kappa."

"As if she asked for it!" Bess declared hotly. This was unbelievable. The sorority was turning into a battlefield. Bess slipped out of the room while the others were arguing and went into the kitchen. She needed something to chew on about now and work off the steam that was building in her. As she entered the kitchen she noticed Soozie sitting at the table, sipping from a bottle of water.

"You know, Kappa is counting on you to get Casey back," she said, her eyes slipping coldly over Bess. "Consider it a pledge assignment."

Bess shivered as her eyes locked with Soozie's,

and she found herself wondering about Soozie's involvement in the whole Brian business.

"I was thinking," Bess said slowly. "As an officer, you probably have some pull with Panhellenic. Perhaps you could talk them into dropping the complaint and convince them to let us resolve the problem with Casey within our sorority. You're probably one of the few people who could pull it off."

Soozie warmed to the flattery. "Maybe you're right," she said. "Well, I might see what I can do." Soozie's cold demeanor surfaced again. "Enough about Casey. Let the other pledges know there's still more clean-up work around here."

Bess grabbed some leftover carrot sticks and chewed viciously as she left the kitchen. How she'd love to tell Soozie off. But there was no point in bringing on more problems. She had enough already, and anyway, there was work to be done.

The pledges were still buzzing about Casey as they resumed their clean-up efforts, but Bess didn't join in the gossip. She worked by herself, hosing the driveway so that she could think. As she washed away the sticky remains of spilled soda, Bess noticed Eileen picking up empty soda cans from around the table where the drinks had been set up. She watched Eileen for a moment, then walked over to her.

"Hi," Bess said as Eileen turned to her. "Listen, Eileen, I've been given a, quote *pledge assignment* unquote, courtesy of Soozie. It's to get Casey to change her mind about quitting Kappa. Will you help me?"

Eileen regarded Bess coolly. "Tell me one good reason why I should help you or Casey?" she retorted, taking off down the driveway. Bess heard the gate slam.

What was that all about? Bess thought in amazement. This whole thing gets more confusing every minute!

Jake awoke in his apartment and stared at the lighted dial of his digital alarm clock. Even for a Saturday, he'd slept late, but he could barely pull himself out of bed. He groaned as he remembered the night before and Nancy's series of disappearances. What was supposed to be a romantic date had become a turn-off date. How had it happened that he'd ended up sharing Nancy with everyone at the party, with scarcely a moment of her time for him?

After showering, he realized he still could hardly keep his eyes open. He grew more irritable as his roommates, Dennis Larkin and Nick Dimartini, joked while they shaved and compared notes.

"I asked Halle what's-her-name out. You know, that cheerleader," Dennis said. He was a handsome jock and never missed a chance to let people know it.

"I got turned down by two girls," Nick replied. "But, hey—better luck next time!"

"You'd better stick to zoology, or whatever that weird stuff you study is, and leave the women to me." Dennis laughed. He flexed a muscle and smoothed back his shiny blue-black hair.

"Hey, Collins, how'd you do with that great-looking babe you took to the Kappa party?" Nick asked, snapping him lightly with a towel as he walked by.

Jake grimaced.

"Ooh, not great, huh," Nick hooted. "What's the matter? Losing your touch?"

Jake left the apartment quickly so he wouldn't have to catch any more flak. When the cool wind outside hit him, he found himself slowly waking up. He walked to Java Joe's, where he ordered a strong cup of coffee to go. Glancing around at the energetic and happy students who were already filling the coffee den, he decided he couldn't deal with their happiness.

He walked out to the quad and sipped as he glanced at the ivy-covered buildings around him. His feet almost automatically carried him toward the building where the *Wilder Times* was housed. Was it only the night before that he and Nancy had good-naturedly agreed not to talk shop for the evening? It seemed like weeks ago. He replayed the scene in Soozie's bedroom several times. What if Nancy hadn't run downstairs? Would he have kissed her and told her how much he was beginning to care? That he was interested in her not just as a fellow journalist, but as something else, too? Would she have said the words he wanted to hear?

Stop it, you idiot—that's a dangerous place to go, he commanded himself, and angrily tossed his cup in the trashcan before entering the building. As he approached the newspaper office, he stopped at the sound of Nancy's voice coming from the hallway. A slow smile spread over his face. He'd come here unconsciously hoping to run into her. Had Nancy done the same? Maybe the day was looking up after all.

But when he turned the corner, he saw that Nancy wasn't alone. She was with Brian Daglian, and when they saw him approach, they became very quiet and acted guilty. What was going on here? Jake did his best to mask his expression. He looked at Brian's gleaming blond head, and for some reason felt like decking him, problems or no problems.

"Hello, Nancy," he said, hoping his voice was steady. "Brian. Didn't expect to see you up after such a night of celebration."

Brian barely nodded hello to him, then, without saying anything more, he grabbed Nancy. "Come on," he said quickly.

Nancy shot Jake a worried glance. "Jake, I'm sorry. I'll see you later." With that, she followed Brian out the door.

"Fine, whatever," Jake said between gritted

teeth. He strode into the newsroom and let the
door slam shut behind him. He'd lose himself in
his writing. It had always worked to block out
problems before. It had better work now.

Nancy jumped at the sound of the slammed
door. If only she could run in and explain it all
to Jake. But there wasn't time, and anyway,
Brian was uptight as it was. She'd just have to
catch up with Jake later and come up with some
explanation that would satisfy him. Nancy followed Brian as he led her up to the lecture halls
on the floors above the *Wilder Times* office.

"In here," Brian said, fitting a key into a lock
and ducking into a darkened lecture hall. His
footsteps echoed as he walked over to flick on
the lights. "I borrowed a skeleton key from one
of my friends who's a teaching assistant for a
class in this room. I don't think my blackmailer
will want to chance being in the journalism building with a bunch of investigative reporters on the
loose," he said, smiling ruefully.

"Probably not," Nancy admitted, sitting in a
hard plastic chair and watching as Brian slipped
the tape into the VCR.

Before long Nancy was viewing the scene between Brian and Chris at Java Joe's. Then the
voice came on demanding money. Nancy sat bolt
upright. Where had she heard that voice before?
It was low and sounded as if it had been altered

electronically. Still, it was somewhat familiar, but she couldn't place it.

"This seems weird, but I've heard that voice before," Nancy said. Seeing the hope on Brian's face, she added, "But I can't remember where."

Brian's expression changed to one of despair. "See what I mean? This is such a mess. When this gets out, my dad's election will be trashed," Brian declared as the tape ended.

Nancy thought a minute, then asked Brian about his dad's political life.

Brian shrugged. "Can't really tell you much," he said. "I've never really paid attention. I guess I was always caught up in school and all. My dad was always traveling, and he was just someone who appeared and disappeared while my life rolled on."

"I just think it would help to know if he had any enemies in particular, or political opponents who might somehow be tied into this," Nancy said thoughtfully, rewinding the tape and viewing it a second time.

"I don't know," Brian replied. "It's almost something of a family joke, how different from my father I am. My relatives razzed me for years, asking when I'd start following in my father's footsteps. I rarely saw my dad's political speeches. I was much more interested in school plays and drama stuff." Brian shook his head.

"My dad insisted I run for student council when I was a sophomore in high school, and I deliberately blew off the election speech. My dad kind of gave up.

"My mom kept after me, though, to at least follow my dad's career. She finally made a scrapbook of articles and photos. Campaign buttons, flyers, things like that. She said, 'One day, you'll want to see what you missed,' I went on guilt overload when I looked through it. I mean, I care a lot about my dad, but I don't want to become him."

"Surely your parents appreciate your own special gifts," Nancy said gently.

Brian shrugged, then nodded. "I guess they do. Lately, at least, they've been encouraging my theater work. Anyway, I kind of felt obligated to bring the scrapbook with me when I came to Wilder. I have it in my room somewhere. I'll show it to you if it would help."

Nancy got up and took out the tape. "Yes, I think that would be a good idea. We've got to figure this thing out and put a stop to this blackmail."

"Tell me about it," Brian said unhappily. "I just dropped this creep another five hundred dollars."

"Don't worry. We'll nail this jerk," Nancy said with more conviction than she felt.

That afternoon Nancy drove her Mustang to town, where she parked in front of the post office. It was quiet for a Saturday afternoon. Still, she couldn't take a chance that she'd draw attention to herself. She slid down in her seat and opened a book, hoping no one would notice her. Every so often she'd look through her binoculars into the large window of the post office, where she could see the row of boxes, including box 2090, where Brian had sent the payments. So far, no luck. No one had ventured near the boxes at all. Nancy was about to give up when she saw Eileen head into the post office.

Wait a minute, Nancy thought. Why would Eileen come here? Even if she had to mail something or buy stamps, there was a postal kiosk on campus, just outside of Hewlitt. Why would she come all the way into town? Training her binoculars on Eileen, she followed her suitemate as far as she could until her view was obscured by two women standing near the post office boxes. Nancy waited until Eileen came back out of the post office.

Score! Nancy thought as she saw that Eileen was carrying an envelope. But she's one of Bess's sorority pledge sisters and my suitemate! she thought in dismay the next second. No time to worry about that, she told herself. She jumped out of the car and hurried toward Eileen. But too late—Eileen was shoving the envelope in her backpack.

"Hey, Eileen," Nancy greeted her.

Eileen smiled distractedly, but she kept walking and Nancy had to jog to catch up with her.

Eileen turned, a look of irritation on her face. "Nice to see you, but I've got to run. I'm really late. I, uh, promised I'd meet someone at the Souvlaki House for lunch," she said, referring to a popular off-campus coffee shop.

"Well, okay," Nancy replied, her eyes drawn to Eileen's backpack. Eileen waved a quick good-bye and took off around the corner.

As she got back into her Mustang, Nancy couldn't help wondering why Eileen was being so secretive. What was in that envelope that she'd so hurriedly shoved in her backpack? Why did Eileen jump about a foot when she saw her? What did she have to hide?

CHAPTER 9

"Hey, good run, Kate," George panted as she and another runner, Kate Terrell, started their cool-down. They'd just completed an extended Saturday training run for the upcoming 10K race.

"Yeah, it was," Kate called back. "Though my shins are a little sore."

"Mine, too. Just call us the pain sisters," George quipped.

Although she joked, George didn't miss the fact that Kate was hardly puffing at all. She sure was in shape, George thought. Well, she'd get there, too. Every day she ran was an investment in tomorrow's strength. She remembered reading that somewhere. But she'd better get there soon, because race day for the 10K wasn't all that far off.

"I hope this Ten-K raises a lot of money for Earthworks," George said, referring to the grass-roots environmental organization that would benefit from the proceeds of the 10K race. George had become a member of the organization the first week of school and was active in the environmental work the group did. The 10K fund-raising race was very important to her.

"I heard the Ten-K last year raised a ton of money," Kate said.

"Terrific," George replied. "I just hope we do as well this year."

"I'm sure we will. The posters advertising the race have been up for weeks. We should get a lot of entries." Kate smiled.

George started to say something else, but then glanced at her watch. "Whoa! I've got to get back and shower or I'll never meet Bess at the Union on time. See you, Kate." With a wave, George headed toward her dorm.

As she showered and changed, George thought about the panic Bess had expressed when she'd asked George to come with her to the Panhellenic Sorority Council. At first George had tried to beg off. It all seemed to be too much of a fuss over how Casey joined Kappa. George couldn't help thinking that this "sorority crisis" just didn't seem to have the same importance as, say, an environmental cause or a world event. Still, Bess was her cousin and friend and Bess needed her, so she might as well help out with something Bess considered important.

Ten minutes later, upstairs in the Union, George spotted Bess pacing back and forth by the window overlooking the quad.

"There you are. I thought you'd never get here," Bess said. She ran her fingers through her blond hair nervously.

"I'm not that late," George protested.

"I know. Sorry," Bess said. "I'm just such a case of nerves. I don't want to do this."

"Relax," George said, smiling at her cousin's dramatics. "You'll be fine. I'm sure the council members are reasonable people."

"Well, one of my friends pointed out one person I recognize who's on the panel. She's from Gamma. They're a pretty cool sorority, with some nice members. I just hope I'm able to get my point across without making a fool of myself," Bess said grimly. "There's a ton riding on it all. Thanks for offering me the moral support."

"Any time," George said. "Where is the meeting?"

"Room 211," Bess murmured, fidgeting as they walked. "Do you think I'm dressed okay?"

George looked at Bess in amazement. Her eyes skimmed over her cousin's simple dark pants and white blouse. "What does what you're wearing have to do with anything?" she asked incredulously.

Bess tossed her head. "A lot. Anything could influence the council's decision. I have to be sure I don't look like a stuck-up sorority girl, but I can't look so casual that it seems like I don't care. It's kind of a fine line."

"Well, to me, you look like any other student on this campus," George said.

"Good. Oh, we're here," Bess said. She turned to George. "Wish me luck."

"You'll do fine. Just be yourself and speak from the heart."

George watched as Bess took a deep breath and opened the door. As they stepped into the room, George caught a glimpse of five young women sitting at a long table. They appeared to be all business. She didn't envy Bess having to speak in front of them. George sat down in the back of the room, hoping they didn't ask her to leave.

Bess was asked to stand at a lectern facing the council. A council member described the complaint: that Kappa sorority had allowed Casey Fontaine to pledge without going through the official rush proceedings and without adhering to deadlines.

"This panel has been called together to explore an apparent violation of the rules as voted on by Panhellenic, which is recognized as the governing body for all sororities," the speaker said.

The council member then explained that the council's role was to review complaints and to make determinations if there were violations of official rules. Finally it was Bess's turn to speak.

"I'd like to start off by saying that all of us at Kappa have tremendous respect for the system," Bess said very softly. "We'd never knowingly violate any rules."

George had to lean forward to hear her.

"The council requests that the speaker please speak up," one of the members said loudly.

Bess darted a nervous glance over her shoulder at George.

Bess has got to state her position more firmly, George thought.

"Project," George mouthed, hoping that Bess got her message before turning back to the panel.

As Bess went on, George heard her gaining momentum. Her voice sounded clearer and stronger. She spoke passionately of Casey's contribution to Kappa's pledge class and explained that Kappa's members were dedicated to fairness, but also felt that sometimes unusual circumstances came up that had to be judged on their own without making generalizations. She wrapped up her presentation by making an articulate case for allowing Kappa to handle the situation within the house.

"It really doesn't directly affect the other sororities, and therefore should be resolved within our own organization," Bess said in conclusion, wiping her forehead.

Good for you, George cheered her silently.

The young woman sitting next to the council chairperson regarded Bess icily.

"There's a word here that we're all having trouble getting around, and that's *fairness*," she began. "Your suggestion that you be allowed to work this out within their own organization has one major drawback. It must be obvious to you that some pledges would feel uncomfortable standing up against opposing viewpoints from upper-class sisters."

"And not every upper-class sister would be happy if pledges spoke against them," interjected another council member.

"That's not true," Bess said in a flash. "I'm a pledge, and I always try to speak up if I don't agree. That's one of Kappa's cornerstones: We all respect one another's opinions, even if we don't always agree."

"Well, good for you for feeling that way," another council member said. "But there may be others who don't have your self-confidence. And those are the pledges we have to consider also."

Bess took a step back and stared wildly at George. It was clear that she didn't know how to counter this.

"I'd like to ask if we are allowed to know who lodged the complaints," she said. "I mean, if they're people who aren't in the sorority system, they might have an ax to grind against the Greek system in general."

The council chairperson stared at one of the other young women. "Well, as a matter of fact, the complaint didn't come from an outsider at all, but from a Kappa pledge. We don't accept anonymous complaints. Her name is Eileen O'Connor."

"Can you believe it?" Bess exploded when she and George were safely out of earshot in the hallway of the Student Union. "I mean, Eileen? We're pledge sisters. We've been through all kinds of stuff together. I never thought she'd do something like this."

"It doesn't make sense," George agreed. "Why would a pledge sister bring this on her own house? Eileen seems like a pretty level-headed person. Not the kind to stir things up just to cause trouble."

"I thought we were so close," Bess continued. "I feel terrible that Eileen wasn't comfortable enough to talk to me and the other Kappas directly if she was upset about Casey's pledging."

"And Eileen had to figure that at some point everyone would find out she was the one who complained," George pointed out.

"Maybe she didn't know her name would be part of an open record," Bess replied. "Anyway, I wonder what Casey will think when she finds out."

"Well, the good news is that you were able to

convince the council to speak with Holly and some of the upper-class sisters," George said. "It seems like the door is still open to resolve this within Kappa before the council takes action."

"I hope so," Bess said fervently. "I've got to find Eileen and talk this thing out before things go from bad to worse. She ought to be in her dorm room about now."

She glanced up at the huge clock tower dominating the quad and felt the blood drain from her face.

"Oh, great," she squeaked. "I was supposed to be at the theater fifteen minutes ago! I've got to get ready for tonight's performance."

She took off for her dorm without a backward glance at George.

"What happened to all of you?" thundered the faculty advisor, Professor Farber, after that evening's performance. He had the cast assembled in the theater auditorium and was pacing up and down in front of them. "You performed wonderfully last night. Tonight you were like robots!

"The night after opening can be a little off because everyone is usually tired from the big night. But there were too many inexcusable mistakes tonight. We've rehearsed for weeks, and I don't want you throwing away all that hard work."

Bess glanced uneasily at her fellow cast members. Everything that Farber was saying was one hundred percent true. The second performance had been one big disaster, from the time the curtain had gone up until it came down. The production crew had glossed over their sound checks, and the microphones hadn't worked properly until the second scene. The cast members had taken several more scenes to regain their momentum. Bess locked eyes unhappily with Brian.

Professor Farber angrily sounded off for a few more minutes, then left the stage. A few of the cast members slunk off to the dressing rooms. Bess and her friends stayed rooted in their seats, their spirits sinking lower by the moment.

"We were everything Professor Farber said and worse," Casey said, her shoulders slumped. "I can't believe that I forgot my place at the end of the first act. Jeez, you'd think I'd know how to do this by now."

Impulsively, Bess put her hand on Casey's shoulder.

"Don't take it too hard," Bess said, trying to buoy everyone. "We've all got a lot on our minds."

Brian stood up. "Maybe we do have a lot on our minds, but I can't believe I missed my cue. I'm letting things get in the way of the show, and this is the most important thing in my life!" He kicked at a pile of stacked chairs in frustration.

Casey got up and declared: "Well, I guess we just have no choice but to make the next performance the best one yet."

After Casey and most of the others had drifted off, Bess looked over at Brian. "This blackmail business is putting you on stress overload," she said softly. "I'm so sorry. I wish we could just catch the money-sucking slime and be done with it."

Brian sat back down on the pile of risers and put his head in his hands. "I tried to block it out of my mind, but every so often I'd look out in the audience and wonder if the blackmailer was out there watching me, plotting the next move."

Bess frowned and watched as a couple of stagehands walked by, carrying scenery. Then she noticed Erik Grenquist loaded down with props. He was carrying a navy backpack over one arm, but his props were so heavy that he set it down by the guys' dressing room.

"You know, maybe now is our chance," Bess whispered. "Do you see Erik's backpack over there?"

"Yeah, so?" Brian looked at her quizzically.

"Let's go check it out," Bess said. "Everyone's got secrets. Let's see what Erik's are."

"We can't go through someone's backpack," Brian protested.

"Want to bet? Watch," Bess said, and moved toward it, Brian reluctantly following her.

"This is all a little too cloak-and-dagger for me," he said, nervously gazing at the door through which Erik had just left.

"You just watch that door," Bess said, hurriedly unzipping the backpack. "Some books, a calculator," she said, rummaging through the contents. "A ticket to a 'Go After Your Goals' seminar? Looks like Erik is into self-improvement, anyway."

"He needs it," Brian said.

"That's for sure."

Bess fished on. Suddenly she exclaimed, "Oh, what have we here? His camera and some photos."

She fished out a small high-quality camera and a handful of photos. Bess gave them to Brian, who squatted down and glanced at the photos.

He started thumbing through them. "These show students around campus, and inside the different places, the Student Union, the architecture building, the library, Hewlitt. These don't prove a thing."

"We're not done yet. Are you still watching the door?"

Brian looked up. "Still watching. Give it up. We're not going to find anything here," he muttered.

"Wait a minute. How about these? You call these nothing?" Bess asked, handing Brian a few more photos.

"Chris and me," Brian muttered. "At rehearsal."

"A-ha! And a blue plastic envelope," Bess exclaimed triumphantly.

"Give me that," Brian said, standing up and reaching for the envelope.

Bess pulled it back from him and studied it

closer. "Empty, but it definitely looks like the others. I think we're on our way to solving this mystery. Won't Nancy be surprised?"

Brian leaped for the envelope again. "I'll get even with Erik. That skinny little dirtbag won't get away with this," he said heatedly.

CHAPTER 10

"There. Done," Nancy said with satisfaction on Sunday morning as she closed down the file in her computer. Her journalism assignment for the next day was complete. Glancing over at her bedside clock radio, she saw that it was almost 10:00 A.M.—time to meet Bess and Brian at Java Joe's. They were going to pool what they had learned.

What to wear, Nancy thought, pausing for a moment before her tiny dorm closet. Something warm, definitely. A look out the window confirmed another cold, gray day. Just as she was sliding into a pair of jeans and a thick flannel shirt, she heard Bess's voice in the lounge. What was she doing here? They were supposed to meet at the coffee bar. Hastily, she combed her strawberry blond hair and stepped out into the lounge.

Bess was talking to Liz, who then disappeared into the bathroom.

"Morning, Bess," Nancy said. "I thought we were going to meet at Java Joe's. Change of plans?"

Bess's eyes were somber. "Sort of," she replied. "Have you seen Eileen yet?"

Nancy shrugged. "No."

Bess stared intently at Nancy. "We've got to talk with her. I found out who lodged the complaint against Kappa and Casey. It was Eileen."

"No. But—but she's your pledge sister!"

"That's what I thought she was."

"Why would she complain?" Nancy was puzzled.

Bess shook her head. "I couldn't believe it either when I heard. I feel so bad. Like I let her down or something. I mean, why couldn't she talk to me if she was upset about everything? She didn't need to do something as weird as going to outsiders to bring up a problem. I was thinking about it all night, and I can't figure out why she didn't trust us enough to hear her out."

Nancy nodded. "I see what you mean."

Bess walked over and knocked on Eileen's door, which Eileen opened, wearing an old high school football jersey. Nancy saw that Reva, her roommate, was gone.

"It's kind of early. What are you guys up to?" Eileen said, eyeing Bess and Nancy with a guarded expression.

Bess drew in a deep breath. "Well, Eileen, I

learned something yesterday, and I just wanted to ask you about it. Why did you lodge a complaint against Kappa and Casey with the Panhellenic Council?"

Eileen's jaw was set, and Nancy could see a small muscle tensing and relaxing in her lightly freckled cheek.

"Lodge a complaint?" she echoed. Then she flicked back her light brown hair.

"Yes," Bess said firmly.

Eileen's eyes darted around. For a second she looked guilty, then she became angry.

"So what if I did? I had every right to," she flashed defiantly. "Anyway, how did you find out?"

"The Panhellenic Council told me. Can we come in?" Bess asked.

Eileen stepped back. "I don't care," she snapped. "Nice of the members to respect confidentiality. I assumed they wouldn't discuss who— well, never mind." She walked over and stared out the window, her back to Bess and Nancy.

"Do you have any idea how it feels to be left out?" she asked after a pause that seemed to last forever.

Nancy's eyes locked briefly with Bess's.

"Well, yes, I do," Bess said, and Nancy could tell that Bess was thinking back to her first days at Wilder, when she'd felt out of step and far from familiar surroundings.

"I've also had times when I've felt out of synch

with things," Nancy said. And thinking of Jake, she added, "And with people."

Eileen whirled around, a sob catching in her throat. "No, I don't think you do," she said angrily. "You turn around and you have a really cute guy like Jake falling all over you. And before him, there were other attractive men as well, Nancy. I really don't think you've ever been left out in your entire life. And, Bess, everywhere you go, men glom onto you."

"What's this got to do with men?" Bess asked, puzzled.

Eileen rushed on. "A lot. And I don't think people like Casey have ever felt out of it, either. People like her have things tailor-made for them. They don't have to follow the rules like everyone else. If they miss a rush deadline, the rules are waived. And if they don't feel like getting their hands dirty cleaning up after a party, well, they don't have to."

"Eileen—" Bess started to cut in.

Eileen waved a hand. "Let me finish. At first I didn't mind carrying an extra load of pledge duties. I mean, I knew you guys were busy with the play and all."

Bess was thunderstruck. "What are you talking about? Eileen, I never meant to slack off. I had no idea you were feeling that way."

Eileen's eyes filled with tears. " 'Eileen, I'm too busy. Do you think you can buy the groceries for the party for me?' 'Eileen, mind if I skip out on pledge work a little early? I have to get to rehearsal.'" Eileen turned back to face the window again.

"And it's not just that," she continued. "I know you're going to think I'm pathetic, but I can't help it. It's not fair that everyone but me has guys interested in them and is paired up. That night at the party, I was just about to start talking with Paul, but he headed right toward you and ignored me completely!"

"Eileen, I didn't know you were interested in him," Bess protested.

Nancy sat still, but finally she asked, "Eileen, did you have something to do with the picketing that night at Kappa?"

Eileen drew in a shaky breath. "No, I didn't. I made the complaint, but I'd never call in people to picket Kappa."

Eileen turned to face Nancy and Bess. Bess's eyes were spilling over with tears.

"Eileen, I must be the worst friend in the world not to have guessed how you were feeling," Bess said. "I just took it for granted that everyone was having as much fun as I was pledging and all."

"Well, I was at first, then things started getting to me," Eileen admitted.

"I wish I'd paid more attention."

"Maybe it wasn't your job to guess how I was feeling," Eileen heard herself saying.

"Oh, Eileen," Nancy said. "It hasn't been easy

for anyone. The whole college thing is new for all of us. I'm not sure anybody really knows what makes college guys tick. We may act like we know what's going on, but inside, all of us are scared."

"I always thought that girls like you two, who seemed to have it all together, never felt weird around guys," Eileen said, and Nancy heard the anxiety in her voice.

"Oh, my gosh, no! I feel weird lots of times!" Bess rolled her eyes, and Nancy nodded in agreement.

"But, you know," Bess said, "it still is fun getting to know lots of guys. When you stop to think about it, not that many people are part of a couple."

Eileen tilted her head and seemed to be considering it. "I guess I just get intimidated easily. And when Casey came along, that just about threw me for a loop. In my poli sci class we were talking about unfairness, and somehow Casey's name came up. Melina—she's our professor— asked us whether it was right to be silent against unfairness. I don't know, but something just went off. So, I lodged the complaint." She hung her head guiltily.

"If it helps any, I felt awful about it right away. I even got a post office box in Weston to send and receive the correspondence I got from Panhellenic so no one would know." Eileen laughed ruefully. "I didn't realize they would make it public.

"I'm going to Panhellenic and drop the complaint tomorrow," she said in a determined voice.

"Who do you think organized the picket?" Nancy asked.

No one had an answer to that one.

Jake was walking past the basketball courts on his way to the newspaper offices when he saw two figures playing one-on-one basketball. Drawing closer, he saw that it was George and Will. They were playing a spirited game, laughing with a closeness that Jake couldn't help but envy. If only he and Nancy had a chance to spend some playful time together. The way things were going, they couldn't seem to spend *any* time together. Jake was struck with a thought: George was good friends with Nancy. Maybe she and Will would know what was up with her. He wasted no time hurrying over to the asphalt court.

"Hi," he said. "Great day for a game."

George looked up and narrowly missed the ball that Will shot. "Yeah," she said. She called out laughingly to Will, "Hey, no fair. It's time-out."

Will held the ball and walked over to Jake and George. The perspiration gave his lean coppery face a light sheen.

"What's up?" George asked.

"You haven't by any chance seen Nancy around, have you?" Jake asked casually.

"No," George said. "I haven't seen her for a while."

Jake stared at his boots. "You don't have to say anything if you don't want to, but is something up with Nancy?"

George's eyes didn't quite meet Jake's. "What do you mean, 'up'?" she asked too innocently. Jake had to stifle the urge to laugh. A good liar she was not.

"George, I mean, is there something on Nancy's mind I should know about?"

Jake saw Will shoot George a puzzled look. "I sure recognize that poker face," Will said, raising an eyebrow.

"Hey," George yelped. "Unfair!"

"It's unfair that I should want to know if Nancy can stand the sight of me?" Jake asked, trying to make it sound like a joke.

"I'll never tell," George said, smiling. "But if it were me, I wouldn't give up on her."

Jake brightened just a little. George might possibly be the world's worst liar, but it was clear that she knew her friend felt at least a little affection for him.

"Be that way," Jake said, but smiled to let her know he was on to her. "See ya around."

He continued onto the library to do some research, his step and his heart just a little lighter.

"There he is!" Bess exclaimed as she and Nancy walked toward the back of Java Joe's.

Brian, who was seated at a booth, raised his head dully when he saw them approach.

"Hey," he mumbled.

"Oh, Brian," Bess said. "I wish this whole thing weren't taking such a toll on you. I can't stand it."

Brian's eyes were bloodshot, and his cheeks were hollow. "You and me both," he muttered. "But thanks. Sometimes I feel like I'm going to become certifiable."

Nancy's heart went out to Brian. No one deserved to feel so terrible. Keeping secrets in could make anyone feel crazy.

"You know," Nancy ventured after the waitress returned with three steaming cappuccinos, "you could tell your parents yourself and save yourself all this worry."

Brian shook his head emphatically. "No way," he said. "I couldn't just break it to them. I don't know how they'd react. I mean, that's a pretty big thing to lay on a person's parents. I've kept my lifestyle secret from them for a long time."

"They'd really be that freaked out if you told them? You don't think they might suspect about you at all?" Bess asked.

Brian shook his head. "I'm pretty sure they don't. We never were a family that could talk about emotional things. Everything has always been on the surface. They'd be so disappointed in me if they knew."

Nancy continued to watch him. She found herself feeling glad she was Carson Drew's daughter. She'd been able to tell her dad anything all her life. Too bad other people didn't feel the same way about their parents.

Nancy sipped her cappuccino thoughtfully. "I know it's absolutely none of my business," she said, "but I can't help but believe that keeping something this significant bottled up inside you is going to make you sick, and will only make it worse when you do talk to your parents."

"I just can't tell them. I'm not ready. I don't know if I ever will be."

As Brian was talking, Nancy noticed a guy a couple of booths away. He was holding a camera. Something about him was familiar. He was aiming the camera at a couple sitting in the booth next to theirs, but then as Nancy watched, he slowly lifted his camera toward them. Then Nancy remembered the name of the guy. She'd seen him opening night—Erik Grenquist.

"Don't look now," Nancy whispered furtively to her friends. "We're being photographed."

Brian's head snapped up. "I've taken about all I can of that guy." With that, he shot out of his seat and, in front of several wide-eyed patrons, leaped for Erik, who shrank back in fear, dropping his camera.

"I've been looking for you, you scum. Why are you trying to ruin my life?" Brian yelled, grabbing Erik's collar.

Erik's eyes were huge. He tried to push Brian off, but his skinny arms were no match for Brian. Watching them in horror, Nancy leaped up.

"Brian, stop!" she shouted.

"Ruin your life? What are you talking about?" Erik sputtered.

"Don't give me that," Brian said menacingly. "You've had it in for me since that night at rehearsal when I accidentally bumped into you."

Erik continued to gape at him, open-mouthed. "Could someone please tell me what's going on here?"

Bess joined Nancy in getting Brian to back off. "Let him loose, Bri," she said.

Nancy and Bess glanced around uneasily at the Java Joe's customers who were seated nearby, watching the drama unfold.

Brian slowly relaxed his grip. "Just make it simple and tell me why, Grenquist," he said.

Erik picked up his camera, and after seeing that it had suffered no harm, glared at his attacker and Nancy and Bess.

"Okay, I admit it: I got really worked up the night you bumped into me. I don't know, something just went off inside me."

Erik looked at the floor. "It's not easy to say this, but I was jealous of the fact that you got a part and I didn't. And so maybe I haven't been exactly nice to you. But just because I took some pictures doesn't mean I'm ruining your life."

"Why *are* you taking pictures?" Nancy demanded.

Erik stared at his pale hands for a few moments. "Well, let's put it this way: Some people get to be the actors in this world, others don't. I realized I didn't get a part in the play because I'm not that good an actor.

"For a while I thought *my* life was ruined. But then I saw that all I needed was a chance to go after some other goals, to be good at something. It happens that I decided to take up photography. I'd like to become good enough at it to maybe work for the newspaper. You gonna cut me out of that chance, too?"

"That's the only reason you're taking my picture?" Brian asked.

Erik nodded. "Yeah. What's the big deal?"

"Nothing." Brian regarded him closely. "Are you sure that's why?"

Erik rolled his eyes. "Cut me some slack, will you. What other reason could I possibly have?"

"I believe him, Brian," Bess said.

Nancy nodded. Somehow, in spite of the fact that Erik wasn't a guy she'd give a congeniality award to, she could sense his sincerity. But something else was troubling her. She could see a blue envelope sticking out of the camera bag that Erik had slung over his shoulder.

"That blue envelope," she said. "Where did you get it?"

Erik took out the envelope. "Student store. They've got these in almost every size. They work great." He opened the flap to reveal the photos inside.

"Oh," Nancy said in a small voice. So much for sparkling detective work, she thought to herself.

"I thought I'd try to submit some candid photos to the school newspaper, maybe the editors would see something they liked, and I might get a chance to join the staff. Is that so wrong?"

"No," Nancy said wearily.

"Now, if you don't mind, I've got stuff to do." Erik picked up his things, and tossing some money on the table, hastily left the café.

As Nancy returned to the booth with Bess and Brian, she watched Erik walk off.

"That's not our blackmailer," Nancy said. "I can't be totally positive, but my gut feeling says he's telling the truth."

Bess nodded, and inspected the grounds at the bottom of her cup. "So Erik's ruled out. Now what?"

Brian shrugged, then walked up to the counter to order another round of cappuccinos.

Bess drummed her fingers on the table. "It still leaves Soozie," she said nervously to Nancy. "I haven't mentioned to Brian that I think Soozie knows about him."

"Yes, we haven't ruled her out completely. We may need to talk to Brian about her, Bess," Nancy said.

"Nancy, the thought that it could be Soozie makes me so scared," Bess said. "How am I, a pledge, going to go after one of the single most influential upperclasswomen in Kappa and accuse her of blackmail?''

Nancy was sympathetic to Bess. As if Bess and the Kappas didn't already have trouble with the Casey problem, she thought. But if Soozie were the blackmailer, then this was going to be a lot more serious than the Casey dilemma.

CHAPTER 11

Nancy, there's no way I can ever confront Soozie if she's the one who's blackmailing Brian," Bess wailed that afternoon as she sprawled across Nancy's bed. "You got a good dose of her. Does she seem like the kind of person who would take kindly to being accused of something this big?"

Nancy looked up from a magazine she'd been leafing through. "Well, we definitely can't say anything unless we know for sure."

Bess added, "I've put so much time into the sorority. All those silly pledge pranks I endured. All the work, and those sleepless nights. It could all just come crashing to an end." Bess buried her face in Nancy's bedspread at the thought.

"Oh, Bess," Nancy said, smiling.

Bess rolled over and spoke intensely. "I just wish it had been Erik. It would have been a real pleasure to wipe that self-satisfied grin off his skinny little face."

Nancy laughed. "Bess, first of all, I think you're being pretty hard on the guy," Nancy said. "You have to kind of admire Erik for trying something else when he realized he wasn't very good as an actor. And second, I think you're being a little melodramatic. Save it for a performance."

Bess listened to Nancy and glared. "Easy for you to laugh. Can you see me, a freshman pledge, taking on Soozie? I might as well kiss Kappa goodbye right now."

"I wouldn't get overheated about that yet. There's still a lot more to be done before we even have to cross that bridge," Nancy replied. "First, we have to establish the connection between Soozie and Brian before we can even get a clue as to the motive. Then we can tackle the issue of anyone's accusing Soozie of blackmail."

"So how are we going to do this?" Bess wondered what could possibly connect Soozie and Brian.

"I just need another opportunity to talk with Soozie," Nancy replied. "The question is, how. I have nothing in common with her. No classes, no clubs."

Bess tried to shut out the music blasting out from a stereo on the next floor while she thought. At last an idea popped into her head. "I've got it! You could pretend you were doing some kind of story for the newspaper!"

"Bess, that's a good idea," Nancy replied. "And I could even kill two birds with one stone. Gail is always after the *Wilder Times* staff to recognize opportunities for news stories and grab them before they get cold. You know, the best stories are often the ones right under our noses."

"So, what does this have to do with Brian's situation?" Bess asked, suddenly worried that Nancy might want to use Brian's unhappy predicament for a newspaper story.

"Why not interview Soozie and get Kappa's perspective on the picketing at the party?" Nancy replied. "I might get an important byline *and* find out if Soozie is our blackmailer."

Bess was relieved and excited at the same time. "Good idea. But there is one catch. Soozie's pretty sharp. There's a good chance she might wonder what you're up to. If she is the one, she'll do her best to throw you off. You might not get anywhere."

"Oh, I think I can handle Soozie. Now, where's my reporter's notebook? Okay, here I go," Nancy said, standing up and tucking her notebook under her arm.

"I'll walk you partway," Bess said. "I have to report to Hewlitt. Professor Farber went ballistic over our performance last night and scheduled an additional rehearsal. I hope we have a better performance at the matinee today."

"You will," Nancy declared.

As Nancy neared the Kappa house she felt her heart start to pound. Dealing with Soozie wouldn't be as easy as she had made it seem to Bess. It would take a lot of finessing not to arouse Soozie's suspicions. She'd have to act like any student reporter wanting to get a story on Kappa's reaction to the disruption of their party by the protesters. She couldn't let on that she was really digging for a different story.

Nancy rang the doorbell and congratulated herself on her incredible luck when Soozie herself answered it. Always decked out in the latest styles, Soozie had outdone herself. She had on an expensive tapestry vest over a silk blouse and black velvet leggings. Her outfit was set off by beautiful vintage earrings. It was obvious that she'd spent a lot of time putting on her makeup, as well. Wonder whom she's trying to impress? Nancy found herself thinking.

"Hi, Soozie. Got a minute? I'd like to interview you for the *Wilder Times* about the events that took place at the Kappa party," Nancy said.

Soozie frowned. "I thought a different reporter was going to do this interview."

"Oh," Nancy said, trying to mask her surprise. Someone had already scheduled an interview with Soozie? Well, she might have guessed that she wasn't the only one around with a nose for news. There were quite a few people on the *Wilder Times* staff trying to impress the paper's editor-in-chief. Nancy tried to cover. "Who did you think it would be?"

The sound of footsteps behind her made Nancy turn around. Seeing who it was, she was surprised.

"Hey, Soozie. Sorry I'm late for the interview," Jake said, hurrying up the front walk. He stopped when he saw that Nancy was there.

Nancy surmised just which reporter Soozie *was* expecting. Think fast, she told herself, frantically racking her brain for anything to help her out of this jam. Then she hit on it.

"You're not late, Jake," she said, giving him a sharp look, her eyes boring into his. "I hadn't started the interview yet." She turned back toward Soozie. "We're *both* interviewing you."

"We are," Jake said, and Nancy hoped Soozie didn't hear the slight question in his voice.

"Yes, we are," Nancy said firmly.

Jake merely nodded.

So far, so good. It didn't appear that Jake was going to blow her cover, but she knew for sure he'd ask for explanations later. What would she tell him? She'd been sworn to secrecy by Brian. Oh, well, time enough to deal with that later.

Soozie led the two of them into the living room, where Jake started asking some carefully prepared questions about the pickets, and Nancy scrambled to make her own questions sound planned and professional. Luckily, it didn't take much work to draw Soozie out. She was eager to talk, and she went on at length about how ridiculous the protest was.

"So much hassle over one girl's pledging. Really, I can't believe how much everyone cares about what Casey is doing. It's no one's business but our own," Soozie said, running her fingers through her blond hair and eyeing Jake in a way that made Nancy grit her teeth.

"Apparently, enough people think it's their business," Jake said. "You had quite a number of protesters show up."

"They completely ruined our party," said Soozie, "which had been going so well. I'd like to find out who they are. I'd let them know a thing or two. I can't imagine what would make people do something so ridiculous."

"Surely you can guess what the other students are thinking—that Kappa bends the rules to suit its needs," Nancy challenged.

Soozie stood up and walked over to the window. She turned around and crossed her arms in front on her chest defiantly. "I don't care what other people think," she said. "What's important is to do what's right for Kappa, and I really think people like those pickets have no right trying to influence our policy decisions."

Jake jotted a few notes in his notepad before asking, "Have you always been this strong-minded?"

Soozie nodded. "It's not easy being in my position, with so much responsibility. Keeping the pledges in line takes a lot of effort. Do you have any idea what it took to bring this party together? The pledges could never have handled it on their own."

"Is it true, as some students charge, that sorority girls are only interested in parties, and that their studies are an afterthought?" Nancy asked.

"No," Soozie declared hotly. "You should see the stack of books on my desk right now. I think that would show you where my priorities are."

Great! Nancy thought. "I'd like to see that stack," she said evenly, not daring to meet Jake's eyes. He must think I'm certifiable right about now, she thought.

"Follow me," Soozie said. "Come on, Jake."

"Sure," Jake said, the corner of his mouth lifting slightly. Nancy could tell he was puzzled, but also amused.

"You're right," Nancy said, making some notes on her notepad after they went up the stairs and entered Soozie's room. "This is definitely a study zone. Have you always considered studies important?"

Soozie nodded and sauntered over to her bookshelf. She picked up her yearbook, and Nancy tried to stifle her flicker of recognition. "See here? Honor roll three years at my high school."

"Let me see," Nancy said, taking the book from her and pretending to examine the picture of the honor guard. Soozie was in the front row.

"I look terrible," Soozie said, darting a look at Jake.

"No, you don't," Nancy said automatically, because she knew Soozie would expect it, then flipped through the book.

"Hey, this is an ad for Councilman Daglian, Brian's father," Nancy added, trying to sound casual. "I didn't know you went to school with Brian."

Soozie frowned. "I didn't. I think Mr. Daglian represents our city, but I don't remember that Brian was at our school. Then again, I didn't really know any of the underclassmen."

"I see," Jake said, though his face plainly said he didn't. It actually said that he was puzzled beyond belief.

Nancy was tempted to ask some more questions about Brian, but she didn't want to appear too interested. She glanced at several more pages, then closed the yearbook and placed it back in the bookshelf.

"What does this have to do with the pickets?" Soozie asked, sounding genuinely confused.

"Nothing," Nancy said quickly. "I have a bad habit of going off on tangents."

"A lot of our cub reporters have that problem," Jake said in a dry tone.

Nancy resisted the urge to punch him in the shoulder. She tried to finish up her questions with Soozie. This was getting her nowhere. If Soozie had a personal vendetta against Brian or his father, she was covering it well. Nancy realized she'd have to figure out some other way to see if Soozie was connected to Brian's blackmailing.

"Well, Soozie, thanks for allowing us to interview you," Nancy said smoothly.

"We appreciate it," Jake said. "Our editor is always asking us to get people-about-campus pieces."

Soozie smiled. "I can't wait to see it. Do you need any photos of me? I've got quite a few good ones."

Nancy stifled her reply to that one.

As Jake and Nancy left the sorority house, Nancy racked her brain trying to think of an excuse for Jake. If only there were an explanation that wouldn't violate Brian's confidence. Any minute now Jake's going to ask what I was doing, Nancy thought.

"Great interview," Jake started. "I'm glad you turned up to help. Surprised, but glad." But Nancy cut him off.

"Let me explain," she said in a rush, though she had absolutely no idea what she was going to say.

Jake shook his head. "Not necessary," he said.

He walked toward the sidewalk without saying anything else. Nancy followed, stopping when he did, by his car.

"See you," he said, giving her a funny look. Then he kissed her on the cheek, got in, and drove off.

* * *

It was late that night when Brian headed for his dorm room. As he walked he shifted his backpack. It was jammed with the books he'd brought to the library. He'd been studying since the matinee ended. For one thing, he'd had a lot of work to catch up on. Because of play rehearsals, he'd fallen behind in his studies. Also, studying helped keep him from worrying about how his life might blow apart at any minute.

When he got to the door of his room, he glanced down and his eye caught the bright blue envelope slid partway under his door. "Oh, no," he moaned. "Not another one." Did this blackmailer ever sleep?

How much would the blackmailer demand now? he thought as he bent over to pick up the envelope. Slipping inside his room, he dabbed at the perspiration beading up on his forehead. His mouth felt dry, and he stared at the envelope for a while. He shoved it under a pile of books and tried to put it out of his mind while he took a shower. He dressed slowly and carefully, stalling for time. Anything to put off the inevitable.

Maybe, just this once, I won't open it right away, Brian thought. I just can't deal with this now. But, no, he couldn't take the chance. The blackmailer usually set swift deadlines.

Dreading it, Brian finally opened the envelope and unfolded a piece of paper. It was a press release with a Post-it note attached to it: Tomorrow this press release will be sent to the newspapers in your hometown. Brian looked on the back, but that was all the note said. No demand for money. Nothing.

Brian leaned against the wall as he read the press release. It was a well-written, detailed account of Brian's gay lifestyle. The author left nothing out. It was obvious that the piece had been researched thoroughly. Whoever had written it had writing style and flair, Brian noted even in the fog of his misery. The release had several paragraphs as to how this news would be received by Brian's parents, the councilman and his wife. Then it went on to guess the reaction of the conservative voters in the district. Brian's eyes began to blur, and a pounding started in his head until he could read no more.

It was slowly dawning on him that the blackmailer had never had any intention of keeping his homosexuality a secret, no matter how much hush money was paid. This release was too spiteful, too well planned. He folded up the press release and sat on his bed, staring at the wall.

What's the use of going on? he thought. My dad's career will be blasted right out of the water, and my mother will never forgive me. Forget acting and all my dreams. I've let everyone down. I might as well face it—my life is ruined.

CHAPTER 12

Nancy sat impatiently as Reva talked with some friends who had dropped by. It was Sunday night, a time when people usually gathered in the suite's lounge to hash over the weekend's events. That night, however, Nancy wished they would all leave.

"Hey, we saw when that guy tried to lay some pretty intense moves on you," one of Reva's friends said.

"Did you see his face when I told him to shove off?" Reva howled.

Nancy joined in the laughter, but still she wished everyone would take off. She stared longingly at the VCR, wishing she were alone and could watch Brian's video.

"Have you and Andy gotten around to any major kissing action yet?" asked one of the women, referring to Reva's computer business partner, Andy Rodriguez. Nancy knew that their "business" partnership had finally turned to a "romance" partnership, and that Reva was very happy.

Reva smiled. "Oh, I'll never tell."

Someone changed the subject to the Internet, and soon the group was involved in a lively discussion of on-line dating.

Nancy listened to the compu-chatter and sighed. Ordinarily, she'd have liked to hear more about surfing the Net, but now all she could do was wish that they had somewhere else to go. Just when she wondered if she'd have better luck calling Bess and seeing if the lounge at Jamison was deserted, Reva's friends slowly began to drift away, Ginny wandered in and watched the late news on TV. Nancy sat and pretended to be absorbed in the latest helpings of mayhem and murder. Finally Ginny yawned and stood up.

" 'Night, Nancy," she said. "Are you going to stay up all night?"

Nancy shook her head. "Just a little while longer. Good night."

At last the lounge was empty. Nancy remained quiet while her suitemates made the usual getting-ready-for-bed sounds. When she was sure everyone had turned in for the night, she slipped the video that Brian had given her into the VCR.

She watched Brian and Chris laughing, and she studied the crowd scene behind them. She didn't recognize a single person except for Brian and Chris. Not that unusual. After all, Wilder was a huge campus. She closed her eyes at the sound of the voice demanding money and tried to see if she could pick up on anything. Though the voice was distorted, Nancy was sure she'd heard it before—but where? She rewound the tape and ran through it again and again without being able to get any answers.

By the time Nancy was on the third or fourth viewing, she had the whole thing memorized. First, there was the slow sweep of the crowd packing Java Joe's. Nobody turned and waved to the camera, so it was obvious that no one had noticed they were being taped. That's strange, Nancy noted. Someone videotaping and no one notices?

There was a slow pan over the coffee counter, and Nancy could see the smiling waitress who sometimes served her and her friends when she came in. Her name was Shelly something. Shelly needed money. She worked at the coffeehouse whenever she could to help pay for her dorm fees. No, of course it couldn't be Shelly, or she couldn't have appeared in the video. Boy, Drew, you're really thinking!

Next came the zoom onto Chris and Brian, sitting in a booth together at the back. They hadn't noticed they were being taped, either. They laughed and talked easily with each other, and Nancy was aware of their closeness. It made her think about her relationship with Jake. If only they could talk and laugh easily. The sad truth was that lately there had been too many things keeping them apart. Hardly the stuff to build relationships. She'd tried to call Jake after the Soozie interview but had only gotten his answering machine. Would she ever get a chance to explain her bizarre behavior?

Nancy sighed. As soon as she'd helped Brian out of his predicament, she'd get to work on patching up her relationship with Jake. That is, if there were anything left to patch. Nancy forced herself to turn her attention back to the video. She listened to the voice demanding the money and played it back slowly. Nothing.

"One more time," Nancy muttered to herself. "I must be missing something."

She continued to replay the tape, feeling more and more frustrated each time. Finally she sat back and tossed the remote onto the low coffee table. It was no use. She was doomed to failure. She stared blankly at the white fuzz that came on the screen.

Suddenly the white fuzz ended and a lecture hall appeared on the screen. The camera came in on Melina Stavros at a lectern. Nancy sat up with a start as she realized a shadowy figure had just entered the room. It was Eileen.

"Boy, Nancy, are you up late," Eileen said. "Why on earth are you watching a political theory lecture?"

"Huh?" Nancy asked. "Oh, it was on the end of something else. I guess someone taped one of Professor Stavros's lectures."

Eileen jerked her thumb at the screen. "Melina tapes *all* her lectures for students who miss them," she replied. She walked down the hall toward the bathroom.

"I see," Nancy said out loud. But to herself she said, Whoever taped the blackmail video over the lecture video didn't realize they'd left part of the lecture. The wheels in her mind were turning. She looked closer at the screen. Was there a connection between a student in Melina Stavros's class and the blackmailer? There would be, if the blackmailer was in Stavros's class. Or could Melina Stavros be involved? But why? A thought came to her. She rewound the tape and listened carefully to the voice again.

Of course, that's it! Nancy thought. The voice on the tape had Melina's distinctive husky tones!

What was Melina Stavros's background before teaching political science? How could she have been connected to Councilman Daglian? Nancy turned these possibilities over in her mind as she shut off the tape and took it out of the VCR. Well, the whole evening hadn't been a waste after all. Maybe she *was* getting closer to the truth!

The next morning Brian burrowed deeper into his pillow at the sound of insistent knocking at the door.

"Go away," he mumbled. He was in no mood to answer. He'd have to get up early enough as it was to attend his Monday morning class. That is, if he went. The way he was feeling, he might not get up at all.

The knocking persisted and grew louder.

"Brian, open up. It's us."

Who was '*us*'? Brian's head was pounding and he was having trouble clearing the cobwebs from his mind.

The pounding continued.

"Okay, okay. Give me a minute, will you?"

Brian crawled out of bed and shivered as his bare feet hit the floor. He slid on some sweatpants and opened the door. Nancy and Bess scrambled into the room and closed the door behind them.

"What's going on?" Brian asked. "I'm not exactly in the mood for company."

"Did we wake you?" Bess asked. "Sorry. We waited as long as we could, but we just *had* to talk with you. It's important. We think we might be closer to guessing who your blackmailer is."

Brian perked up. "Who is it? I guess that's the question for the day, isn't it?"

"Do you know that political theory professor Melina Stavros?" Nancy jumped in.

Brian brushed his hair from his eyes and sank wearily onto his bed. Where was this coming from?

"No, I don't," he said irritably. "I'm not taking any classes like that."

"Listen, I know you probably think we're completely crazy," Nancy said excitedly, "but I'm sure we're onto something. I don't have much to base my hunch on, but I think Melina Stavros might be your blackmailer, or connected with the person somehow. And I need you to check it out. Remember that scrapbook you told me about, the one your mom made for you?"

Brian nodded slowly. He could use a cup of coffee about now. He jerked his chin in the direction of his bookshelf. "Down there, next to those play books," he muttered.

Nancy pounced on it. She sat on the end of Brian's bed and thumbed through it. Brian watched as she studied each page intently. When she came to the end of the scrapbook, she frowned.

"Well, maybe I was wrong." Sighing, Nancy bent over to pick up a campaign ribbon that had fallen out of the book onto the floor.

"Sorry," she said.

"Don't worry about it," Brian said. "Some of that glue doesn't hold too well."

Nancy flipped to the center of the book and tried to locate where the ribbon had come from. Then she sat up and pointed at a newspaper clipping.

"What a minute!" she exclaimed. "Check this out."

Bess scurried over for a look.

"That's her, all right," Bess said.

Nancy got up and showed Brian a photograph of a young Melina Stavros, standing with a group of people lined up in front of a red, white, and blue Bob Daglian for City Council banner. She looked so earnest and serious.

"So? That's an old campaign photo," Brian said. "I don't get it. Who's 'her, all right'?"

Nancy ran her finger across the caption. "It says here, Melanie Stowe."

Brian looked puzzled for a minute, and then his face darkened. "Melanie Stowe. I'd forgotten about her. She used to be on my father's staff. That was years ago. But then she was fired—for stealing."

"Tell us about it," Bess prompted.

Brian stared at the photograph of the young woman. "I don't remember much about her. Like I said, I wasn't all that involved in my dad's campaigns. But I do remember that he was pretty upset about what had happened with Melanie. He'd really worked hard to groom her. He told me later that she had the charisma to become a political powerhouse herself. At the time, I thought he was saying that to point out that I wasn't made of the same stuff."

"So, your dad fired her after he found out she was stealing from him?" Nancy asked.

Brian nodded. "He could have taken the easy way out and had someone else do the firing. But my dad's not like that. He told me he confronted her himself, and he gave her a chance to confess, which she did."

"Serious stuff," Nancy said.

Brian was quiet for a moment before adding, "My dad used to talk about how betrayed he felt. He'd encouraged her so much, and then she went and threw it all away. Funny, I've been so out of it that I've probably seen Melina around campus and never recognized her. I guess it just didn't make a deep impression on me."

"It evidently left a deep impression on her," Nancy said grimly.

"Yes, I guess it did. So you really think it's Melanie or Melina or whatever she's called?" Brian asked.

"It seems like a good bet," Nancy answered. "She has motive and she has opportunity."

Brian was thoughtful a minute before he spoke. "I just got another note under my door last night," he said. "This one's the real thing, all-out revenge. There wasn't even a demand for money. Melina's going to send a press release out today telling my hometown newspaper everything."

Nancy stood up. "We have to go to her office and try to get in. We need to find something that we can use to prove she's your blackmailer. We'll just have to take a chance on not getting caught."

Brian paused. "I'd go with you, but I made up my mind last night that I can't live like this anymore. I've got to call my parents and talk to them right away before they read about it in the paper. I'm going to tell them everything, about the blackmailing and what you suspect about Melina being involved—and about Chris and me. I'm afraid if I don't do it now, I'll lose my nerve."

No one spoke for a few seconds, but finally Bess broke the silence.

"All right, Brian," she murmured. She stood up and placed her hand supportively on his shoulder. "Remember, no matter what, you're our friend."

"Good luck," Nancy added.

I'll need it, Brian thought when they left. He picked up the phone and began to punch in his home phone number.

"Poor Brian," Bess said as she and Nancy hurried out of the dorm and started toward the political science building. "He's going to be a basket case before all of this is over."

"It's all so awful," Nancy said.

"I don't get how people can be such complete jerks," Bess replied.

"I don't understand it, either. How some people can hate for such a long time," Nancy said.

"What I can't get over is that people can't move on and get over it," Bess marveled.

Nancy nodded in agreement. "It is startling to see how people can obsess over something that happened years ago."

When they got inside the political science building, Nancy looked on the directory by the front door. "Melina Stavros. Room 323. Third floor."

"Boy, this building is deserted. It's so early that no one's around for classes yet," Bess added.

The two women stepped into the elevator, and once on the third floor, they located Room 323 right away. Turning the doorknob, Nancy was surprised and relieved that it was unlocked.

"Odd," she said. "But, hey, I'll take a break. I don't need to waste time with a lock pick."

She and Bess stepped into the dimly lit interior of the office, and it took a few seconds for their eyes to adjust.

"Jeez, her office is almost as big a mess as my room," Bess said.

Nancy took in the piles of paper stacked everywhere and the books spilling out of the bookshelves. How would they ever find anything in this mess? Nancy wondered as she started leafing through papers on the desk.

"Check out this ugly print," Bess said, peering at an old woodcut of some unnamed political figure. "Who is this guy anyway?"

Nancy ignored Bess's chatter. "Come on. We don't have time to lose. Try those papers on that credenza by the window."

"I'm looking, I'm looking. Hey, do these look familiar?" Bess asked. She tossed a couple of empty blue plastic envelopes over to Nancy.

"Well, they do seem to be turning up everywhere. Having the envelopes in her office could be one piece of evidence linking Melina, but they aren't enough. The student store probably had a sale on them, so she bought a bunch," Nancy said, examining them, then setting them down.

Nancy and Bess continued digging through the papers. They had to hurry. Any minute now students and professors would start filling the hallways and they'd lose their chance to find the evidence they needed to nail Melina.

"Hey, I found something!" Bess called.

Nancy hurried over, and Bess held up an ivory envelope—addressed to a newspaper in Brian's hometown.

"Big mistake, Melina Stavros," Nancy said, taking it from Bess. "We just found what we were looking for."

The next instant the door flew open.

CHAPTER 13

Both young women jumped, and as Nancy turned, she found herself peering into the face of Melina Stavros, who walked purposefully into the room.

"What are you doing in here?" she asked, her dark eyes flashing.

"We'd like to talk to you about this." Nancy thrust the envelope in Melina's face.

Melina's mouth gaped open, and she dropped her briefcase on her desk. "Give me that," she commanded.

"I don't think so," Nancy said, jerking the envelope away.

"Give me that, or I'll call security," Melina thundered. "Breaking into a professor's office is grounds for expulsion from the university. You can forget any thoughts of getting a degree from Wilder."

Bess tossed her head. "I don't think you want to call security."

"You might be forced to do some explaining a lot sooner than you might have thought," Nancy added.

"I don't know what you're talking about," Melina said.

"I'm betting you do," Nancy replied. "And it involves blackmail."

That stopped Melina.

"What do you want?" she asked after a pause, eyeing Nancy and Bess.

"Some explanations," Nancy said simply.

"I have nothing to say."

"Oh, I think you have plenty to say." Nancy stepped in front of the office door and closed it firmly.

"We know all about what you've been doing to Brian Daglian," Bess chimed in.

"Brian who?"

"Nice try. Try again," Nancy said.

"Oh, come on. I told you I have no idea what you're talking about."

"We think you've been blackmailing Brian. We've seen the notes and photos. And we have a videotape that was sent to Brian. That tape was made over one of your lecture tapes. The end of that tape still has a segment showing you in one of your lectures," Nancy said.

Melina became flustered, then quickly recovered. "Everyone knows I tape all of my lectures for anyone who may have missed a class," she said. "Dozens of students have copies of my videotapes."

"I wonder whose fingerprints the police may find on the notes and photos Brian has been getting?" Nancy stared hard at Melina, but the professor didn't flinch. Boy, she's one tough lady, Nancy thought.

"This is ridiculous. Why in the world would I be blackmailing someone I don't even know?" Melina sounded annoyed.

"Oh, you know him all right," Nancy said. "Does the name Melanie Stowe mean anything to you?"

Melina paled a bit, and small beads of perspiration appeared on her brow.

Bess spoke up. "Brian is calling his parents right now and telling them everything. Councilman Daglian will get to the bottom of this. And he'll make sure you're prosecuted for what you've been doing to Brian," she said boldly.

At the sound of the councilman's name, Melina flushed angrily. But Nancy thought she also saw a trace of fear. Melina opened her mouth to say something else but evidently thought better of it and finally sat down heavily in her office chair. She stared with unfocused eyes at a picture that was hanging over her desk. It was of Melina shaking hands with a foreign dignitary. She was quiet for quite a while before speaking.

"I was on Bob Daglian's staff," she began, "and Bob used to say that I had a future in politics. I didn't need him to tell me that. I could see it for myself, because I had respect and power. I'd been with the campaign for a few months when Bob put me in charge of the campaign funds. The other staffers were jealous that I had so much responsibility. But I thrived on it." Melina smiled slightly.

"Unfortunately, I never was very good at handling my own money. It always slipped through my fingers like water. You have no idea how expensive it is to be a 'servant of the people.' You have to entertain, to dress right, to be able to pay your own way to events. I was always in debt, and the campaign fund was too tempting. I did it in such a way that I thought nobody would ever guess the money was missing. No one would have known. It was just a temporary loan, and I was going to pay it back as soon as I could—"

Nancy interrupted her. "But you got caught first."

Melina paused and stared at Nancy. "I tried to explain that I would pay it all back, but no, our councilman was a total Boy Scout. Said honesty was a quality he valued above all others. Blah blah blah. He said he was sorry for me, and then, just like that, he fired me," she continued. "I mean, fired. Ha!" Her laughter had a hollow ring, and the shadows from the morning sun played eerily across her face. "Bob didn't have to fire me. Do you understand what that meant? He ruined my career."

Nancy watched Melina, feeling anger and pity for her at the same time. What a mixed-up woman. She didn't seem to care about what she had done.

Melina was going full steam now, her words coming faster and faster. "There I was, without a job or any references. No political future at all. Ruined. So I started over.

"I moved and changed my name back to the original Greek family name. My great-grandparents had changed it to Stowe from the Greek Stavros when they first came to America. Land of the Free. Oh, sure," Melina said with great bitterness. She stood up as if she were commanding a lecture hall, her voice rising. "Did you hear me? Land of the Free, I said."

Nancy didn't dare breathe. She stared with a terrible fascination at the wreck of the woman before her. Melina Stavros, one of the most popular professors at Wilder. It didn't seem possible!

"Go on," Nancy urged.

Melina's eyes focused and she returned to her story. "I set up a new life for myself. Ended up here at Wilder. Not the worst place I could have ended up, actually. I mean, everybody liked me. Students were dying to get into my classes. I could forget about my past and my dreams and get on with my life."

"Then why would you want to hurt Brian?" Bess burst out. "I mean, you sound like your life was happy here. Why risk all that?"

Melina stared at Bess with an expression Nancy couldn't read.

"One day at the beginning of the term, I saw Brian walking through the quad. He was a younger version of his father. A blond arrogant god, expecting people to throw roses at his feet. I don't know—something went off inside me—rage at what Bob Daglian had done to me." Melina's face was twisted with anger.

"I wanted to hurt Bob somehow for what he'd done to me. I noticed that Brian was always hanging around with Chris Vogel, and there was something about the way he and Chris were when they were around each other. So I began to watch them whenever I could. From their actions toward each other when they thought they weren't being observed, I realized Brian and Chris were more than friends."

She looked at Nancy, but Nancy was conscious that it was more like Melina looked *through* her.

"So then what?" Bess asked.

"The more I saw him around campus," Melina went on, "the more I realized he was not 'out' about himself with very many people. And I wondered whether Brian's family knew about him. It occurred to me that his parents might not know.

Bob Daglian hated having his perfect world disrupted.

"I got to thinking. Bob Daglian happens to be from a very conservative district. There are a lot of people who wouldn't take kindly toward this little bit of news. So I found a way to hurt Bob, through his son. First squeeze the son for a little cash, then announce my news to everyone, right when Bob was up against a tough campaign. The news would sink him."

"How could you? Brian is such a wonderful person. He never did anything to you," Bess cried out.

As if she didn't hear Bess, Melina continued, "I decided to take a chance and see how much it might be worth to Brian not to have his folks in on his little secret. I was right. Brian sent me the money immediately."

Melina stopped and glanced at Bess and Nancy. "The money was nice and all, but what I really wanted was revenge on Bob Daglian. It had been a long time, but Melina Stavros doesn't forget. I planned from the first to leak the news no matter what. I can't wait to see what our esteemed councilman has to say when the whole world knows his son is gay, because let me assure you, that press release is going out."

She laughed in a way that gave Nancy a chill. Melina's eyes looked wild and she gestured wildly. "You two are crazy if you think I'm going to let you ruin my plan—or what I have going at Wilder."

George and Pam walked through the academic quad on their way to their first class.

"It's perfect running weather. Cool, clear." Pam groaned. "I wish we weren't stuck inside today."

"I know what you mean. It's a drag when classes get in the way of the fun we could be having," George joked.

"Sure you don't mind swinging by the poli sci building? If I don't turn in this paper, I won't get credit," Pam explained. "I was lucky Melina gave me a few days' grace. She can be a stickler for turning work in on time."

George shrugged and glanced at her watch. "No problem. It's still pretty early. We've got plenty of time."

As they started up the stairs, George found her thoughts drifting to Will. Things had been going so well for them lately. After a rough start, her relationship with him was now settling into place. Classes were going well, too, and she was feeling more and more ready for the big 10K coming up. George wasn't sure when she'd been happier.

It wasn't until they neared Melina's office that George became aware of the sound of raised voices. That's odd, she thought. It was still early, and so far she and Pam seemed to be the only ones around. As they drew closer, the hair stood up on the back of her neck. She raised a warning finger to her lips. Pam shot her a puzzled look, but she slowed down and walked quietly toward the office. Both young women froze as they heard Melina's voice raised shrilly, and the low undertone of someone answering.

"Someone's in there with Melina," Pam whispered. "I hope she's not in trouble or something."

George bit her lip. "I feel weird barging in, but I can't help feeling that something is going on."

With that, she threw open the door, just as a briefcase came flying at her head.

"Look out!" Nancy cried, and George ducked. The briefcase crashed against the doorjamb.

"Nancy! Bess! What's going on?" George gasped, gazing at her friends.

"Melina!" Pam exclaimed.

Melina Stavros hurtled by, shoving George and Pam out of the way. George could hear her footsteps tearing at breakneck speed down the hall.

"Call security!" Bess said, reaching for the phone herself.

"What is going on?" George demanded.

"We found our blackmailer," Nancy explained to George.

Later that day Bess sat backward in her chair at her desk and looked at George, Nancy, and Brian, who were all in her dorm room. Remembering that Leslie would be gone most of the day at physics lab, Bess had asked her friends to stop off and unwind after classes so they could talk over the day's events.

"Pretty unbelievable, huh?" she asked, passing around a bowl of popcorn.

Brian was sitting on the floor, and he spoke first. "I want to thank you all for everything. I don't know what I would have done if this had gone on much longer. I thought I was going to explode—not to mention go broke."

"Not a problem," said Nancy. "Thank George for her fortunate arrival—and for deflecting the briefcase. I'd probably be in the student infirmary about now if she hadn't barged in at the perfect time."

George was sitting cross-legged on Leslie's bed. "It was good that we alerted the police in time to stop Melina before she got away."

"The police were glad to have the photos and notes as evidence," Nancy said. "Along with our statements, it was enough to detain her."

"Melina's students will be in for a shock when this hits the campus paper. And wait till it all goes to trial," George said, thinking of Eileen and all the students who enjoyed Melina's classes so much. "Talk about negative publicity for Wilder U."

"This definitely was a no-win situation all the way around," Nancy agreed.

Bess turned to Brian, compassion filling her eyes. "How about you? You okay?"

Brian nodded slowly. "Yeah, I'm okay. Telling my folks wasn't actually that bad, although I was shaking like crazy while I dialed their number."

Bess nodded. "It must have been nerve-racking. No wonder you were freaked. How did they take the news?"

"All things considered, they were okay about it. I was totally surprised. I guess I expected shouting and carrying on, or maybe an overdose of 'How could you do this to us?' My mom just got kind of quiet, and then said that she would always support me in everything I did. I'd hoped that would be how she'd take it, but I couldn't be sure."

"What about your dad?" Bess asked quietly.

"The funny thing was, he acted like he already knew. I think maybe he's known or suspected for a while." Brian cleared his throat before going on. "Anyway, they told me they loved me and that nothing could change that."

"Oh, Brian, I'm so happy for you!" Bess exclaimed, her eyes shining with tears.

Brian nodded. "Thanks. We talked for a while and they were really supportive. It made me feel like the weight of the world had been lifted from my shoulders. And then I told my folks about how we suspected Melina as the blackmailer, and my dad went ballistic. My mom calmed him down, though."

George leaned back against the wall and put

her feet on Leslie's bedspread. "All's well that ends well," she said happily.

"It won't end well if Leslie comes back and sees that you've messed up her perfectly made bed," Bess pointed out.

Brian smiled. "Where is Ms. Perfect Doctor Woman anyway?"

"Dr. Wannabe is lost somewhere in physics land and probably won't be back for hours," Bess said.

Bess and her friends laughed. Leslie was legendary for being a neatness freak. Bess had always wondered how fate had conspired to match Leslie, queen of neat, and herself, major-league mess maker, as roommates. There was just no explaining some things.

"Wait till I tell Chris that this whole nightmare is over." Brian grinned happily.

As everyone talked, Bess found herself thinking that although she was happy things had turned out well for Brian, she still had some problems of her own simmering. Namely, the Casey and Kappa problem.

"Well, now that we've solved Brian's dilemma, maybe I can tap all the brain power in this room to help me figure out what to do about Casey and the sorority," she said.

Catching her friends' bemused looks, she added defensively, "Well, it's important to me!"

"We know it is," George said.

"Bess," Nancy said, "I've been meaning to ask you, how does Casey feel about all this?"

"I think she's embarrassed to be at the center of so much controversy," Bess admitted. "She doesn't want anyone to be troubled on her account, so she figures the only way out is to quit. But I really don't think she wants to leave Kappa and all her friends."

"She shouldn't have to quit if she doesn't want to," Brian pointed out.

Bess nodded. "That's how most of us feel, but it still comes down to the unfairness thing. Some of the pledges feel that if their friends who were part of rushing didn't get invited to pledge Kappa, why should Casey be allowed to sail in when she didn't even go through the rush process?"

The door to the dorm room opened. "Rushing sororities. Now, there's a scintillating topic," Leslie said, her voice dripping with sarcasm as she came into the room. Her eyes swept over George, who jumped up guiltily.

"I thought you were in the physics lab," Bess said.

"I finished ahead of schedule. What cute pledge pranks are you dreaming up now?"

Bess felt her cheeks heat up. In the past she had just taken it when her roommate dished out her venom. But lately she'd begun to stand up to Leslie.

"I don't know, Leslie," she said. "You're so smart. I'm sure you have all the answers."

Leslie narrowed her eyes. "Whatever," she said. She flipped on her study light and opened one of her textbooks. "Just dream up your little sorority doings quietly. I have work to do."

Bess looked over at her friends and rolled her eyes, but then a revelation hit her. There *was* a way to resolve the bad feelings among the pledges and get Casey to remain in the sorority. She had to talk to Casey right away—before it was too late!

CHAPTER 14

Is everyone here?" Bess asked, glancing around the lounge in Jamison Hall, where the pledges were gathered after she had summoned them for a secret emergency meeting on Tuesday afternoon.

"Looks like we've got everyone," Eileen said. Bess could tell she was uncomfortable, even though earlier Bess had assured her she'd smooth over any talk about her filing the complaint against Casey.

"What's the big secret?" asked one of the pledges. "Are we in more trouble?"

Bess looked around the room. Most of the pledges were eyeing Casey, who was sitting on the armrest of the sofa.

"You want to explain?" she asked Casey.

"I think you've all guessed the topic," Casey

said, standing up. "So let me make this easy by starting off and saying that I'm sorry about involving everyone in this whole pledging mess. I completely understand if you don't want me in the sorority. I can just quietly send in a resignation, and then I'll just pledge some other time."

There was silence in the room, which was broken when one of the quieter pledges, Kim, stood up and cleared her throat.

"I for one want to see Casey stay in Kappa," she said. "I don't see what the big deal is." She glared defiantly at everyone and sat down.

Several more pledges agreed, but then someone spoke up from the side of the room. "Well, I'd like to see Casey stay, but we still can't get around the fact that she didn't have to go through all the stuff that we did."

Bess's eyes met Casey's. "I think we have a solution. I talked it over with Casey, and she's agreed to go through a pledge prank of her own. We don't have to tell anyone. It'll be our secret."

"All right!" chorused several of the pledges.

Kim stood up. "So what does she have to do? We all went through some fairly dumb stuff. It only seems right that Casey do something humiliating."

"I propose we have Casey serve breakfast in her pajamas to the guys at one of the fraternities," someone proposed.

"Too easy," protested someone else. "And besides, then everyone would know about the secret pledge prank."

The pledges ran through a number of ideas, each rejected for different reasons. Bess thought they might never agree on what to have Casey do for a prank, but suddenly she had an idea.

"I propose we play Truth or Dare, only we change the rules," Bess said. "We each get to ask the questions or pose the dares to Casey."

"I don't know," Casey said, suddenly looking as if maybe she'd bitten off more than she could chew.

Bess gave her a penetrating look. "No one said it would be easy," she said. "I think it's a good idea. But it's your choice."

Casey smiled. "Okay. Okay. I can handle it."

The pledges gathered in a large circle and Casey sat cross-legged in the middle.

"Truth or Dare," began the first girl.

Casey bit her lip to keep from laughing. "Truth."

"Is it true that you slept with Charley Stern while you were still filming the pilot of your TV show?"

Casey's cheeks burned, and Bess wondered if they'd started off a little too ruthlessly. But then Casey lifted her chin and nodded.

"Truth or Dare?" challenged Kim.

"Dare," Casey said, this time a little more uneasily.

"I dare you to tell us what you really thought of the guy who played your ex-boyfriend on the show. What was his name? Derek Blaine or something?"

Casey put her hands on her hips. "Not fair! That's more a truth than a dare!"

"We never promised it would be fair," pointed out one pledge. "Tell us."

"Fine," Casey replied. "I had to act like I liked him, but he had the worst breath, and I begged the scriptwriters not to make me kiss him on screen again."

The pledges burst into laughter as Casey wrinkled her nose. Bess could see that she was warming up and getting into the spirit of the game. "Who's next?"

"Truth or Dare?" This time it was Eileen's turn.

"Was it true that you also slept with Derek while you were dating Charley Stern?"

"Guess again," Casey stated emphatically. "Derek spread that rumor because he kept hitting on me offstage and I told him to try his line on someone who cared," Casey said. "He lied to the Hollywood tabloids about us being an item. But I got back at him." Casey grinned wickedly.

"He was freaked about the fact that I was taller than he was, so one day I hid the platform shoes he wore for our scenes. We were filming this cliffhanger scene for a big two-hour special, and he appeared on screen about five inches shorter than me. It was in all the rag sheets the next day. He wanted to crawl under a rock, which is where I always knew he belonged. The worm!"

By now the pledges were shrieking with laughter. Finally one last pledge asked a question.

"So, Casey, do you ever feel superior to people your age because you're a famous actress?"

The smile left Casey's face, replaced by a hurt look. "No," she said.

"Truth!" someone shouted.

"I am telling the truth," Casey said, her voice half the strength of what it had been a few seconds earlier. "Actually, sometimes I felt a little guilty because I've had so much success at such a young age. I've met really amazing people. Most kids my age haven't had these experiences."

Bess noticed that the room had become still, as everyone listened attentively to the beautiful actress. Casey looks so vulnerable, Bess thought.

"Why did you go into acting, anyway?" Eileen asked.

"The truth?" Casey looked up for a moment. "The truth is that I was bitten by the acting bug when I was in high school. I played the part of Rizzo in a high school production of *Grease!*, and that was it, I loved it. I wanted to be an actress so bad that I drove my parents crazy begging them to let me audition for something. Finally an open audition was being held in my hometown of Springdale for a commercial, and my aunt took me to it. I got the part and landed an agent, and bingo, before I knew it, I had the part in *The*

President's Daughter and was off to Hollywood."
Casey paused.

"I got off track for a while out in Hollywood.
I was so famous that there were a lot of people
who wanted to be friends with me. I started running with a really fast crowd, you know, going to
clubs, that scene. Charley tried to get me to stop,
but I wouldn't listen."

Again there was silence in the room. This was
a side of Casey that no one had ever been allowed to glimpse before.

"I thought the people in the club scene were
my friends, but they really only liked me because
I was famous." Casey shook her head and continued. "My parents were afraid I'd become your
basic kid-in-Hollywood story, so they got me
some counseling. I realized there was still so
much I didn't know about the world. Suddenly
acting didn't seem so important anymore. I
wanted to find out about other things, so I applied to college. I was accepted at a number of
schools, but my parents wanted me to come here
so I'd be far away from the Hollywood scene."
Casey took a shaky breath and looked around
the room.

"We never heard about that," Eileen said.

"Anyway, I guess that's why I want to be in
Kappa so much. I want to be friends with all of
you because I want to just be accepted for me,
not some famous actress."

Bess smiled as she looked around the room.

The other women were all watching Casey with a mixture of caring and respect. This Truth or Dare initiation had done more than make up for Casey's having missed rush and early pledging. It had helped bond them together as friends, including Casey.

Impulsively, Bess hugged Casey. "You *are* our friend—our sister—and nothing will ever change that." Suddenly all the pledges gathered around Casey and swallowed her up in a collective bear hug.

Walking into the Student Union, Nancy dumped her heavy backpack on the floor by a cluster of sofas and dropped down into a chair. She'd just spent the morning in her journalism lecture, she and her fellow students getting grilled by the professor on ethics in journalism. She felt as if she'd held her own, but now she was exhausted. It would be fun meeting up with her friends for light conversation.

Across the room, she spotted Dawn, who was talking earnestly to a couple of students seated at a table. There was a sign hanging from the table, but Nancy couldn't make out what it said. Wonder who they are? Nancy thought vaguely as she waved and Dawn waved back. Probably some student political group or students with a new cause. Whatever, Dawn looked happy, and Nancy was glad that Dawn was starting to make an effort to get involved in Wilder life again. Dawn had pretty much shut herself off from the world in the aftermath of a broken romance. Getting involved in something would do her some good, Nancy decided.

Nancy smiled when she saw George and Will approach, hand in hand. Once again, she couldn't help but notice how comfortable they were together, as if they were born to be a couple. Nancy felt a twinge of jealousy and tried to stuff down the uncomfortable fact that she couldn't seem to make her own romances work.

Oh, Jake, she thought. I've probably completely blown it with you. And here I'd promised myself when I started at Wilder not to let mysteries get in the way of my life here.

"Hey, how's it going?" Nancy greeted George and Will.

George grinned and slid onto the sofa across from Nancy. Will sat beside her. "No complaints. I just survived my first paper for my crazy professor in philosophy."

Will ruffled her hair affectionately. "You did a great job on it. I read it."

"Well, I didn't put that much time into it, I was so busy with my training runs," George admitted. "And the professor is legendary for being a tough grader. I'm just glad I didn't totally get blown out of the ballpark. How about you, Nan? You look whipped."

Nancy shrugged. "Nothing some time with my friends won't cure," she said.

A few moments later Bess, Casey, and Eileen arrived and joined the group. Soon they were all laughing and talking. After a while Nancy's attention was caught by a group of women standing by the bulletin board, watching her group. Nancy was sure she saw one of the girls pointing at them. Now what? she wondered, as the group started advancing slowly toward her and her friends.

"It's just not fair, it's just not fair," they started to chant, causing other students milling around the center to stop and stare. It was the same slogan the pickets had chanted the night of the protest at the Kappa party, Nancy realized. Their voices grew steadily louder and the tension began mounting.

Nancy darted a look at Bess, Eileen, and Casey, who were frozen, watching the advancing group.

"Unreal," Bess whispered. "Not again. Will this never end?"

"Back off," Eileen shouted, standing up and facing the group. "Get your faces out of our business once and for all. We've already settled it among ourselves!"

Then, unbelievably, the protesters started laughing.

"We're glad you've settled everything," one girl said, stepping forward. "But frankly, we couldn't care less. We just came to tell you that we're from Pi Phi, and we were forced to picket your party as a pledge prank. Hope we didn't mess up your opening night too much."

"What?" cried Bess.

"My name's Montana Smith," the girl said, holding out her hand to Bess. "We weren't going to say anything, but I couldn't stand your not knowing that it was all part of a prank."

"What?" Bess sputtered again. Then she smiled and shook her head as she realized that she and her friends had been had.

"Well, you're pretty good actors," Nancy said, laughing. "You had us fooled. My roommate Kara's in Pi Phi, and she never let on for a minute."

Montana nodded. "I know, she was sworn to secrecy. We kept Kara out of the picketing, because we figured you might guess it was a prank. The upper-class sisters forced us to make it look real."

"Too bad you didn't pledge Kappa," Casey added. "We can always use more performers."

"Well, actually, we Pi Phis are more into the environment and all," explained one of the other girls. "But it was kind of fun making our acting debuts at Wilder."

Will shook his head. "You had us all going."

"I never had a clue," George exclaimed. "And I've been working with some of the women from Pi Phi. They're the sorority that's been helping the Earthworks group plan the Ten-K run fundraiser."

"Well, anyway, we just wanted to clear things up. We promise we'll make it up to you. Okay?"

Bess looked at her pledge sisters and nodded. "Okay. Just don't let it happen again," she said with mock severity.

"We'll see you all at the race next week," Montana said as the Pi Phis left.

"Well, that clears up another mystery," Nancy said, and stood up and stretched.

Speaking of mysteries, here comes Jake, she thought as he walked into the room. Her heart turned over as she took in the way his burgundy sweater set off his lean, well-muscled body. He stopped for a moment to talk with someone.

"Nancy, you're staring," Bess said under her breath.

"Yeah, maybe I am," Nancy admitted.

Jake looked up from his conversation and made eye contact with Nancy. Soon he was on his way over to the group.

"Hi, everyone," he said as he approached. But he reserved a special smile for Nancy.

Nancy was startled to realize how happy she was to see him. She hadn't talked to him after the interview with Soozie. And Jake hadn't called, either. But now he was smiling at her. Maybe things weren't completely blown after all, Nancy thought hopefully.

"I've been at the *Wilder Times* office, talking with the faculty advisor," Jake said, "and Gail Gardeski—about you."

Nancy sat up. "About me, why?" she asked curiously.

Jake looked at her. "Can't say."

"Jake!"

"It's a secret."

Nancy slumped in her seat. There was nothing she could say. After all, she'd been the queen of secrets since she'd met Jake.

Jake turned away, as if to go. Great, thought Nancy. He drops this mysterious secret on me and then leaves. I have all the luck!

Abruptly, Jake turned back and in one quick movement gave Nancy a long, deep kiss. He stood there, leaving Nancy feeling breathless.

"There, I've been wanting to do that all week," Jake said, and taking Nancy's face in his hands, looked directly into her eyes. "Now. You and I have a date for dinner tonight, and then tomorrow night, and the night after that, and maybe the night after that. And I don't want to hear any more excuses about your being busy, all right?"

Nancy was almost speechless with shock and happiness. "All—All right, whatever you say." She smiled shyly. "Dinner sounds great."

Jake nodded and gently touched her cheek, sending an electric current of excitement shooting through Nancy. He winked and smiled, then walked away, his cowboy boots rapping against the floor.

"Whew! He sure perked you up," George said, grinning.

Nancy smiled in agreement as she watched Jake go. She couldn't believe what he'd just done. But she loved it. She'd always known that Jake was cute, as well as talented and funny. Now Nancy realized that he was mysterious and unpredictable as well. She had a feeling that in this relationship she'd never know what was going to happen. Relationship? Yes, it looked as if she hadn't blown it after all. Dinner tonight with Jake. Nancy shivered with anticipation. So much for mysteries getting in the way of her life at Wilder!

NEXT IN NANCY DREW ON CAMPUS™:

In training for the upcoming 10K race, George is working up a heavy sweat, determined to do well and ensure her qualification for the track and field team. But at times winning can be deceiving, and Nancy's beginning to wonder if her promotion at *Wilder Times* is on the up and up or if Jake's been pulling strings. Speaking of deception, what's the deal with REACH? Dawn Steiger has already joined the group, which promises to work for peace and understanding, but Nancy suspects REACH has a different goal, and she's out to get the story. Bess, meanwhile, wants to know Paul Cody's story: Is he for real or just another guy out for a good time . . . in *False Friends*, Nancy Drew on Campus #7.

Christopher Pike presents . . .
a frighteningly fun new series for
your younger brothers and sisters!

The creepiest stories in town. . .

1 The Secret Path
53725-3/$3.99

2 The Howling Ghost
53726-1/$3.99

3 The Haunted Cave
53727-X/$3.99

4 Aliens in the Sky
53728-8/$3.99

5 The Cold People
55064-0/$3.99

By Christopher Pike

A MINSTREL BOOK

Published by Pocket Books

Simon & Schuster Mail Order
200 Old Tappan Rd., Old Tappan, N.J. 07675

Please send me the books I have checked above. I am enclosing $_____ (please add $0.75 to cover the postage and handling for each order. Please add appropriate sales tax). Send check or money order–no cash or C.O.D.'s please. Allow up to six weeks for delivery. For purchase over $10.00 you may use VISA: card number, expiration date and customer signature must be included.

Name _____

Address _____

City _____ State/Zip _____

VISA Card # _____ Exp.Date _____

Signature _____ 1175-01

Now your younger brothers or sisters
can take a walk down Fear Street....

R·L·STINE'S

GHOSTS of FEAR STREET

1 Hide and Shriek
52941-2/$3.50
2 Who's Been Sleeping in My Grave?
52942-0/$3.50
3 Attack of the Aqua Apes
52943-9/$3.99
4 Nightmare in 3-D
52944-7/$3.99
5 Stay Away From the Treehouse
52945-5/$3.99

A scary new series for the
younger reader from R.L. Stine

A MINSTREL® BOOK
Published by Pocket Books

Simon & Schuster Mail Order
200 Old Tappan Rd., Old Tappan, N.J. 07675
Please send me the books I have checked above. I am enclosing $_____ (please add $0.75 to cover the postage
and handling for each order. Please add appropriate sales tax). Send check or money order–no cash or C.O.D.'s
please. Allow up to six weeks for delivery. For purchase over $10.00 you may use VISA: card number, expiration
date and customer signature must be included.

Name _____

Address _____

City _____ State/Zip _____

VISA Card # _____ Exp.Date _____

Signature _____ 1180-01

Nancy Drew on Campus™

By Carolyn Keene

Nancy Drew is going to college.
For Nancy, it's a time of change....A change of
address....A change of heart.

Nancy Drew on Campus™#1:
❏ New Lives, New Loves......52737-1/$3.99

Nancy Drew on Campus™#2:
❏ On Her Own....................52741-X/$3.99

Nancy Drew on Campus™#3:
❏ Don't Look Back................52744-4/$3.99

Nancy Drew on Campus™#4:
❏ Tell Me The Truth.............52745-2/$3.99

Nancy Drew on Campus™#5:
❏ Secret Rules...................52746-0/$3.99

Nancy Drew on Campus™#6:
❏ It's Your Move.................52748-7/$3.99

Archway Paperback
Published by Pocket Books

Simon & Schuster Mail Order
200 Old Tappan Rd., Old Tappan, N.J. 07675
Please send me the books I have checked above. I am enclosing $_____ (please add $0.75 to cover the postage
and handling for each order. Please add appropriate sales tax). Send check or money order--no cash or C.O.D.'s
please. Allow up to six weeks for delivery. For purchase over $10.00 you may use VISA: card number, expiration
date and customer signature must be included.

Name _____

Address _____

City _____ State/Zip _____

VISA Card # _____ Exp.Date _____

Signature _____ 1127-05

NANCY DREW® AND
THE HARDY BOYS®
TEAM UP FOR MORE MYSTERY...
MORE THRILLS...AND MORE
EXCITEMENT THAN EVER BEFORE!

A NANCY DREW AND HARDY BOYS SUPERMYSTERY™

- ☐ DOUBLE CROSSING — 74616-2/$3.99
- ☐ A CRIME FOR CHRISTMAS — 74617-0/$3.99
- ☐ SHOCK WAVES — 74393-7/$3.99
- ☐ DANGEROUS GAMES — 74108-X/$3.99
- ☐ THE LAST RESORT — 67461-7/$3.99
- ☐ THE PARIS CONNECTION — 74675-8/$3.99
- ☐ BURIED IN TIME — 67463-3/$3.99
- ☐ MYSTERY TRAIN — 67464-1/$3.99
- ☐ BEST OF ENEMIES — 67465-X/$3.99
- ☐ HIGH SURVIVAL — 67466-8/$3.99
- ☐ NEW YEAR'S EVIL — 67467-6/$3.99
- ☐ TOUR OF DANGER — 67468-4/$3.99
- ☐ SPIES AND LIES — 73125-4/$3.99
- ☐ TROPIC OF FEAR — 73126-2/$3.99
- ☐ COURTING DISASTER — 78168-5/$3.99
- ☐ HITS AND MISSES — 78169-3/$3.99
- ☐ EVIL IN AMSTERDAM — 78173-1/$3.99
- ☐ DESPERATE MEASURES — 78174-X/$3.99
- ☐ PASSPORT TO DANGER — 78177-4/$3.99
- ☐ HOLLYWOOD HORROR — 78181-2/$3.99
- ☐ COPPER CANYON CONSPIRACY — 88514-6/$3.99
- ☐ DANGER DOWN UNDER — 88460-3/$3.99
- ☐ DEAD ON ARRIVAL — 88461-1/$3.99
- ☐ TARGET FOR TERROR — 88462-X/$3.99
- ☐ SECRETS OF THE NILE — 50290-5/$3.99

Simon & Schuster Mail Order
200 Old Tappan Rd., Old Tappan, N.J. 07675
Please send me the books I have checked above. I am enclosing $_____ (please add $0.75 to cover the postage and handling for each order. Please add appropriate sales tax). Send check or money order--no cash or C.O.D.'s please. Allow up to six weeks for delivery. For purchase over $10.00 you may use VISA: card number, expiration date and customer signature must be included.

Name _____

Address _____

City _____ State/Zip _____

VISA Card # _____ Exp.Date _____

Signature _____ 664-13